STEP INTO FREEDOM

BY

PERRY WATKINS

COPYRIGHT

DISCLAIMER

I am a person in long term recovery from alcohol and drug abuse. I used the twelve steps of Alcoholics Anonymous to get and stay sober after thirty-five years of alcoholism and drug abuse. I have spent years reading and studying self-help books and have spent countless hours watching videos on personal growth. I have completed courses including Tony Robbins Personal Power. I am a public speaker and a volunteer who speaks and tells the good news that recovery is possible for everyone. I am not a health care professional. I am not a psychiatrist or a therapist. I am not a counselor or a medical professional. I hold no legal qualifications of any kind.

TABLE OF CONTENTS

CHAPTER FIVE: FOR THE LOVE OF FOOD
INTO THE FRYING PAN
A TRIP AROUND THE WORLD

CHAPTER SIX: THE DIFFERENCE MAKERS PART 2
BONES
DANCING WITH THE DOPE MAN
BIG GIRS DON'T CRY
LOVE AT FIRST PUFF

CHAPTER SEVEN: THEY OUGHT TO PUT IN THE WATER PART 2
FIND YOUR PASSION
LOSE CONTROL
RE-TRAIN YOUR BRAIN

CHAPTER EIGHT-DIFFERENCE MAKERS PART 3
BLACKOUT TO BREAKTHROUGH
GRANDMA'S GARDEN
KATZ DANCE
SHE USED FOOD
A MESSAGE FROM GOD

   IN CLOSING

DEDICATION

This book is dedicated to Gina DeBiasi my significant other for over thirty years. She has stuck by me through thick and thin. This book would have not been possible without her help and sometimes tough love. She has been my rock.

INTRODUCTION

In this book you will read about people who have endured unimaginable trials and who have overcome mental and physical scars, loss, grief, pain and despair. Although their struggles have been different, they all share something in common; they survived, and they thrived.

If you are struggling with any area of your life you may be able to find a solution using a twelve-step recovery program and simply replacing what that program is focusing on with what you are struggling with. It can be just as simple as replacing the words to fit your issue.

As you read their stories you will also read something more important, something deeper and more powerful that will hopefully guide you from a life of struggle to a life of victory.

By successfully using a 12-step program each person who had lived a life of addiction was able to move from the initial step of acknowledging their powerlessness to the final and most rewarding step of practicing these steps in their daily lives.

They are winning and you can to. Give this a try and you will be amazed at the results.

CHAPTER ONE

THE PARENTS

"Spoons Are For Stirring Coffee, Dad"

When Danny was in a good place in his mind, his indicators were obvious. His eyes were aglow; they sparkled and twinkled like polished stones. His smile proved that the law of attraction was real. When his smile was in full bloom, others couldn't help but be drawn into his happiness.

We all tried. Everyone reached out, everyone was on his side, everyone prayed he would come out of it, but the toxins of his disease always won. Our love and compassion were never enough, which proved that his demons were running the show. In the end, our hearts were riddled and torn from our sense of failure. The loss we felt should not have surprised anyone.

Danny's early home life, as well as his early school days, were difficult at best. He was one of those kids who was sweet as he could be when everything was going his way. However, as we all know, that isn't reality. Danny was hyperactive and out of control much of the time. Though he was medicated for his Attention Deficit Disorder, his behavior was wild and unacceptable. An act of authority from anyone was met with immediate refusal. Danny rejected his teachers' and his mother's demands to behave. These were the warning signs of things to come.

By the time Danny was 11 or 12, he was smoking pot and drinking. It is unclear when he turned to harder drugs. It wasn't long before the pattern of using drugs to change how he felt became ingrained in his spirit.

Sometime during this period, Danny tried everything he could to alter his consciousness. He was fond of huffing anything he could get his hands on. Huffing is concentrating a toxic substance, such as spray paint or computer cleaner, in a paper sack, covering your face with the sack, and inhaling the toxins into your system. The main ingredients were cheap and readily available. Gasoline was one of Danny's favorites—and one of the deadliest. The ramifications of huffing on a still-developing brain run the gamut from severe learning disabilities to a long-term coma or even death.

When Danny was 16, tragedy struck. While driving around partying with his girlfriend and friends, Danny was involved in a horrific car wreck. He was thrown through the back window and suffered a severe closed head injury. He had to be life-flighted to an area hospital and was in critical condition. It's cliché but true; Danny's dad got the phone call that parents dread. The doctor on the other end of the phone said, "Mr. Smith, you need to get here as soon as you can. Your son is fighting for his life." Danny somehow managed to pull through and recover from his injuries but not from his need to feel different or to feel nothing at all.

The results of the accident, along with his drug abuse, laid out a dark and twisted path forward in Danny's life. He would never be the same, which made it even more difficult to defeat his personal ghosts. What happened next happens all too often. The doctors prescribed Vicodin and Oxycontin for pain. With Danny's established tendency to use drugs, this escalated to heroin use almost immediately.

Because of Danny's long-time drug abuse, his mind drifted relentlessly. He struggled at times to accept his confusion, making it difficult to determine whether the space between his thoughts was the truth or something he imagined.

Danny felt like he was being pulled in and out of a bad dream. The delusional nature of this can cause synesthesia. This is a phenomenon in which the senses are confused. For example, a person can taste color vividly. They can look at a metal object and get a metallic taste in their mouth. Perhaps Danny tasted black, the color of darkness. The taste in his mouth may have confused him. He had battled every day to keep his life from being engulfed by the king of darkness, and it may have been difficult for him to distinguish the flavors.

Danny's life ran toward nowhere and everywhere at once. He moved about and gravitated from one tragic event to another. He steered his life in any direction depending on the taste in his mouth. He couldn't wash out the taste of defeat and became convinced that he deserved all of it.

Danny hated needles so his stepsister shot him up with heroin for the first time. He described the feeling to his dad: "It felt like having 100 orgasms at once." However, it doesn't take long before that feeling of ecstasy is gone. The obscure conversation in an addict's mind is addiction.

The first time Danny overdosed, he was in a parking lot, where he lay lifeless. His face took on a shade of blue that came from the inside but appeared on the outside. The foam running from his lips reaffirmed his condition. The second OD confirmed to his dad that Danny was truly a heroin addict. His dad went into his room to wake him up. Danny was lying there with his body in a state of suspension, lifeless and cold. His dad tried to shake him out of it while he waited for the paramedics to arrive. They told him that when he shook his son, Danny's body had reacted to the stimulus, which may have saved his life. This trip to the hospital was just one of many to come. From his early 20s and for five straight years, Danny went to 22 different rehab facilities and inpatient treatment centers.

Danny had been locked up and arrested so many times, his dad can't remember the exact number. On one of his last arrest, he was put in the drunk tank that held many other prisoners. Danny launched himself into a rage so unmanageable, the deputies on duty had to come in and take him down to the ground. They took him to solitary confinement and stripped him down to his underwear. Danny was strapped to a chair and the door was slammed shut, leaving him to his madness. The deputies had no idea that Danny was like a magician. His arms and wrists were double jointed. He manipulated his joints and, in a flash, was out of the straps and out of the chair. What they also didn't realize was that during the scuffle, one of the deputies had lost his name tag, which was now in Danny's possession.

Free from the chair and with his fractured mind reeling, Danny cut himself. He attempted to cut off his scrotum using the dull name tag. It was apparently sharp enough to partially cut him; he managed to cut enough to expose and drop a testicle, creating a gruesome sight for the guards who rushed in trying to stop him. He was taken to the hospital and placed on suicide watch.

Once Danny was released, he would have his time in court. The sheriff pleaded with the judge to send Danny to a secured mental institution and not to jail. His men had seen a lot of things, but Danny's self- mutilation had rocked them. The judge sentenced Danny to nine months in a locked-down mental institution in the hopes that Danny would get the help he needed.

Nothing would take hold and nothing anyone could do helped. Danny was now approaching his late 20s and had given up on his life. He struggled for so long and went through so much hell that he lived a life much older than his 27 years. His day-to-day ability to do anything, including the simple things, was akin to that of swimming through mud, with each stroke harder than the last. His loved ones could see in his face the toll that his life of addiction and mental illness had taken. Hopelessness is a real thing, and it lived in Danny's room.

On the evening of August 26, 2017, his dad hugged him and asked, "What's wrong?"

From somewhere deep in his soul, Danny replied, "I'm tired."

His dad didn't realize that Danny had given up and that the response "I'm tired" meant that Danny was tired of it all. He was tired of the constant fight within himself—a fight that he never won. He was tired of the shame that he perceived was real from having let everyone down. He was tired of the constant voices that lied to him saying, "You're no good and you are worthless to the world." No, his dad could never have known.

Sometime during the night, Daniel Smith's physical body let go of its pain. His glimmering eyes, which had once sparkled, dimmed past the darkness. Now stoic, they took one last look at Danny's soul before it escalated toward the God of his understanding and his salvation. I imagine the lights of his spirit rushing toward its holy and blessed destination.

I see it all in my imagination with remarkable clarity, and I am convinced of its truth. My vision sees a lightning bolt in reverse, picking up speed and color as it is shot from the earth toward the heavens. Danny's spiritual presence was riding along like a cowboy, saddled up and strapped down to the endless spectrums of color and light. Danny arrived at his destiny with a bang, our loving God welcoming his precious angel with all his love, mercy, and forgiveness. It is a warm and comforting vision that should make us all feel the love of the creator of the universe.

On the morning of August 27, 2017, Danny's dad looked in on him. The needle still in his arm did all the talking. His beautiful son, whom he loved so much, was gone. His sorrow isn't unfamiliar to others who have lost their children to this horror.

The shock and pain come first, then the guilt of feeling relieved that it's over.

I know Danny's dad personally. Danny and his dad regularly attended recovery meetings that I had the honor of chairing. His dad stood beside him through thick and thin and never left his side. His commitment speaks to the caring love this man had for his son.

We all loved this kid, and we were all powerless to overcome his demons. At his memorial service, stories were told about his good times and not about his addiction. We all cried and loved one another. The kids on my left and right joined with their peers behind me, holding each other. I felt honored to be there and to speak words of encouragement to them. They had all felt the devil's curse through their veins, and all were in different stages of recovery.

Danny's dad, Mike Smith, held his head high and received the love that we were all sending him. He spoke to the audience and tried to uplift everyone. This unselfish act was his way of trying to help others grieve through their loss.

Daniel Smith lost his fight with addiction, but his dad will not be silent about it. Mike Smith spent years trying to help his son. He now shares his story with others in the hopes of touching those who feel hopeless. The title of this story comes from a conversation Mike had with Daniel. Mike recalls Daniel saying to him, "Spoons are for stirring coffee dad." "Not for burning down heroin."

Mike Smith got off the bench of years of struggle. He stepped up to the plate of personal loss and hit a deep fly ball into the endless space of hope.

I want to thank my dear friend Mike for having the courage to share Daniel's story. The life lesson is clear. Mike refused to take on the role of victim. He won't miss any opportunity to speak to the world about addiction. He shares ways to overcome loss and the miracle that is recovery. The steps of acceptance have taken hold in Mike's heart.

POSITIVE FURY

With all we now know about prescription pain pills and heroin, they are no longer ghosts in the darkness.

Andy was a great kid. He was charming and loving, and his teachers thought highly of him. They could see the sparkle in his eye, a sparkle that shined brightly into a future of promise. He was popular and well-liked by his peers. Throughout his youth, his home life was excellent.

Andy was as normal as any small-town kid in America. He lived in the type of small town where everyone knows your name. Norman Rockwell would have painted this landscape of peace and security. This was a tight-knit community that embraced its children as if they belonged to everyone. No one in the community could have seen the dragon's breath of the hell that was about to enter their backyard. It was a hell that would touch Andy's life, as well as the lives of other beloved young people in the town.The local drug dealer had left behind a horrible plague that afflicted not only Andy but an entire community.

One night, Andy was at a party with his buddies. Like some of the other kids, Andy experimented with prescription pain killers. He felt comfortable, as painkillers weren't like the street drugs he was committed to never using. It made Andy feel good. However, his habit progressed until just a little was no longer enough.

Andy went on to complete his studies and graduate from high school. His friends did the same. They hung around together, doing what young men do. They partied, dated the ladies, and appeared to be heading in a normal and correct direction. A few had already given into their addiction, which raised some eyebrows in the community, but it didn't feel like a five-alarm fire at this point.

Andy began to work and save his money. Although he was using drugs, he wasn't so lost that he couldn't function. It appeared from the outside that Andy was on the right track. He saved up for a car and was acting responsibly in his words and actions. The metamorphosis that was taking place in Andy's life would stun everyone.

His father was a local business owner who employed his son and began teaching him the trade. It all felt so natural and right. Being a loving and caring parent as well as Andy's boss, he began noticing subtle changes in Andy's behavior. He became concerned but never thought of a drug problem. His father assumed Andy's behavior was part of growing into an independent young man.

This inappropriate and totally out-of-character behavior began to worsen to the point of greater concern. Finally, Andy had a confrontation with his father in the driveway of their home. His father asked Andy, "What is going on with you? Do you have a drug problem?" Andy instantly denied that he had a drug problem and sped out of the driveway. A few minutes later, Andy came back and in a very emotional state, admitted to his father that he had a problem with oxycontin.His father was relieved that it wasn't the heroin that he had heard about.

What his father didn't know, and what Andy later revealed to him, was that Andy had very quickly left behind the oxy and was shooting heroin.

With this lack of this knowledge, Andy's dad had no reason to research all that is now known. He admits that his thoughts were, 'We'll send him to a rehab facility and Andy will get the help he needs. The old Andy will be back. It'll be a hard lesson to learn but he certainly won't get involved in this type of behavior again.'

That was far from what happened. Andy suffered relapse after relapse and was in and out of different facilities, all to no avail. Andy attended multiple 30-day programs as well as 90-day programs but he always started using again.

As his addiction grew, Andy sold his belongings, lied to his loved ones, stole from his family, and did anything he could to get what he needed. As a result, he was constantly in trouble with the law and ended up in the legal system.

During a surprise test, Andy tested positive for drugs and his probation officer turned him into the judge. Andy received 90 days in jail for violating his probation. After doing most of that time, Andy was released. To his father's delight, Andy looked great and started acting like his old self.

Slowly and guardedly, his father started putting Andy back to work. However, like many addicts, Andy suffered from depression and had "up" days and "down" days. The people who love the addicted wake up in the morning on pins and needles. They live in the hope that this will be one of those "up" days.

Andy woke up one day severely depressed. Trying to fight his way through it, he went to work under the supervision of a trusted employee. His father continuously checked on him throughout the morning and was obviously concerned. It was clear that Andy was down. When questioned by his dad, he replied: "Nothing can cheer me up."

Unknown to his father, Andy had brought to the job site a new, unopened PlayStation. Andy made a phone call to a drug dealer. The dealer showed up and Andy traded the PlayStation for heroin. It is hard to comprehend what Andy must have felt like; he had fought so hard and now was about to give into the vicious demon that screamed in his mind.

Around 2:00 p.m., a co-worker noticed that Andy wasn't around. Andy's friend and foreman on the job began looking for him. He ended up at the porta-john. They found the door locked and no response from the inside. Quickly, they pried open the door to find Andy unconscious. The foreman immediately started CPR while another called 911.

Then came the most dreaded phone call any parent of an addict can receive. The voice on the other end said, "You'd better get to the job site." His father asked, "Is it Andy?" The response was yes.

When his father arrived on the job site, the first responders were working on his beautiful son. He watched the life of a promising young man slip away into the wind and into God's hands. On May 17, 2010, Andrew Hirst left this life on earth.

He sprouted angel wings and left the torment of his earthly bonds. Our tears flow freely, but in our hearts, we must know he has kissed the face of God and felt God's mercy with the promise of peace that lasts forever.

Positive Fury – Andy's father, Mike turned his grief into a term he calls, Positive Fury!

The first three days after the shock of losing his son left Mike uncharacteristically silent. His family had been crushed. That's when Mike made a decision that would change his life forever. He was going to stare this evil in the eye. He wasn't going to live like a victim. He was going to make a difference. Mike stepped up to the plate and decided to go to war with the enemy that had taken his son and so many others. He spoke at his beloved son's funeral. He spoke of loss and hurt but also of hope for those who are still suffering.

His funeral was attended by Andy's friends, some of whom were addicts. One of the young addicts told Mike that they didn't know if they would be welcome. Mike's response was simple: "Of course you are. You're the ones who need to hear this."

Some of the addicts, like Andy, lost their battle in the months to come. Some, as a result of this tragic loss, got clean and sober and are now living wonderful, recovered lives.

Mike was far from done. He began educating himself on heroin addiction. He read everything he could and talked to everyone he could. He went to local group meetings and met the local sheriff and the county prosecutor. He spoke and asked questions of educators and of people who worked and volunteered in the recovery world. He soaked in any information he could. He, in fact, not only stepped up to the plate but also swung at every opportunity to learn.

Mike is a very successful businessman. He is upbeat and positive. He wants to tell the world what is possible for people who are in recovery. He wants this so much that he formed a group called Andy's Angels.

The mission statement of Andy's Angels is to educate the community on opiate abuse and to provide support for families and those still suffering from addiction. Look up Mike Hirst's bio and information about Andy's Angels by searching online for the Face Book Page- Andy's Angels.

Mike has spoken to Congress and has spoken before state legislators and judges. He never stops giving of himself to help raise awareness.

Mike is currently working on refurbishing a large complex in his community for people in recovery to live and thrive in their community. He is always willing to go the extra mile. He decided to take the pain of his loss and turn it into a phrase he coined: POSITIVE FURY.

Mike got off the bench of devastating loss, stepped up to the plate with positive fury in his heart, and swung at the problem, hitting it all the way to the halls of Congress.

Mike is powerless to bring back his son, but he isn't powerless over his grief. His faith brought him through his darkest hour. That same faith has made him shine.

ALAN'S SONG

Multiple atrocities are committed against children throughout this country and the world. Some are hidden in our society, but not this time. Alan told his story.

The three-year-old Alan cried and screamed as if he were seeing the devil through the car window. His father stood there with a puzzled look on his face. His mother said to her ex-husband, "No way this kid gets out of this car and goes in that house with you." Something was very wrong, and she sped away. Once they were out of sight of the house, the boy calmed down. His mom and his sister, who was also in the car, asked him what had happened that had scared him so much.

Openly and calmly, Alan told the story of the sexual molestation that his father had committed against him. Alan's mother had immediately taken him to the police department, where he was questioned separately by two sets of experts in the field of child molestation. The boy's story never changed. Alan's natural father was banished from his life. This was a hidden scar that lurked in the recesses of his memory for the rest of his life.

Alan V was gifted at school; his teachers liked him, and he was popular. His changes in behavior were hardly noticeable. The only clue that something was about to happen appeared when Alan was in eighth grade. He filled an empty water bottle with vodka and drank it on the school bus. He was caught drunk at school, and his actions were written off as a stupid mistake. The common phrase, "Boys will be boys" was used to explain it away.

Alan's hometown was like many others in those days. The town did not realize that a heroin epidemic was coming. The epidemic was sneaky at first, lying in wait to gain strength.

That's what evil does. If it comes into the light too quickly, it raises too many eyebrows and is often removed before it can take hold. So, like a panther, it sits calmly on a cliff above the town, twitching its tail back and forth in anticipation. It is patient and it waits until it has infiltrated all cultural and economic classes. When the time is right, it lunges off the cliff in plain sight. It kills as many as it can before it is held at bay, but only for a moment. There is a public outcry to law enforcement to cage the beast, but the infection has taken ahold of its victims and no cure is immediately available. The cure is awareness and education, but that takes time.

Alan liked alcohol, and so did his friends. Many who start drinking at an early age do so to cover up some type of pain in their lives. Drinking alcohol was his catalyst. Soon he was off and running, trying everything he could to change the way he felt about himself. No one can pin point an exact reason people start to use substances to change how they feel.

At 17, Alan became a heroin addict. The days of only getting drunk and smoking dope were over. Alan wanted to stop, but unfortunately the ever-growing addiction, the daily lies, and the theft to get the drugs his body and mind needed had become his second nature.

Alan's family tried to help him get on the right track. They often came to his rescue in the hopes of a miracle. They bought an old car that he could use to get back and forth to jobs that never lasted.

Alan's mother tells a story about an old car that Alan had once driven. Worn out, it had been reduced to scrap and was headed for the junkyard. Alan told his mom to tell his stepfather to look in the trunk before he sold the car. Alan said, "He's not going to like it." When his stepfather opened the trunk, he found a nearly complete meth lab inside it.

Alan's mother and stepfather bought him another car. It was an effort to help him find a job and go to work. Alan returned home one night with no car and a suspicious look in his eyes. Alan claimed that he had been at a party when he was assaulted, tied up, and forced to sign over the title to the car. The culprits drove off in Alan's car, which was never seen again.

Over the years, Alan was in and out of multiple recovery centers. He always left with a good but false attitude. It was the "I got this now" type of attitude, which doesn't work. Alan's triumphs were short-lived and his struggle with addiction continued.

Through a chance meeting with a minister, Alan's mother was directed to a local recovery facility called Teen Challenge. It was a faith-based recovery facility and program. She and Alan went to his interview for placement in the recovery center. Alan's mother desperately tried to convince the counselor to accept him into the program.

Alan was now in his early 20s, and the hard life he had created had taken a toll on his attitude. His remarks during the interview were detrimental to his case and his mom begged relentlessly to overcome the counselor's every objection to Alan's placement. She begged for what she felt was one last chance to save her son's life. The counselor finally agreed to let Alan enter the program.

Alan was right where he needed to be, and everyone involved experienced a glow of relief. Alan was doing well and seemed to be on his way to a sober life. He fit in and was liked and accepted. With Phase One of his recovery complete, Alan was sent to the next phase of his recovery to a recovery center several hours away from his home.

Once again, Alan did the work and earned precious family time off campus so to speak. His sister and her husband came to pick him up for the weekend. At this point, Alan had been clean for months. His family was relieved; it was like the burden that they had carried for so long had sprung a leak and was getting lighter every day. When they arrived, Alan made up an excuse to bring all his belongings along for the weekend. It wasn't until they were miles away that Alan disclosed the truth about why he had brought along all his things from the recovery center: He wasn't going back.

Once home, Alan headed down the road of heartbreak all over again. For a while, he kept his promise to not use drugs or alcohol. His mom got through each day looking to find some good in his return. The truth was, in her heart she knew otherwise.

Alan's routine on his way to relapse was predictable. It started when he hooked up with his old buddies. Then Alan started drinking alcohol. His empty shot glass always ended up in another type of "shot"...a shot he would stick into his arm, a shot that would lead to his final day on earth.

His friends were dying all around him. Heading into his final days, Alan told his mom that they were doing it wrong. He told her that the mistake they were making was getting clean for a while, then trying to shoot up the same amount as they had before they got clean. Alan said, "Mom, I'm smarter than that."

On May 29, 2015, at the age of 24, Alan James Kenneth Vaughn left his pain behind. He had joined the thousands of others who had fought the same battle and the same demons.

A call came to his mom late on a Friday night. Her daughter's voice was on the other end of the line. "I think Alan has died," she said.

Shock, disbelief, and denial ran through his mother's mind. She said, "That can't be. I just talked to him this morning on the phone. He's coming over tomorrow to help us move."

Her daughter replied, "I think it's him. It's all over Facebook. They're reporting a death due to overdose on his street."

When Alan's mom and stepfather arrived at Alan's house, the yellow police tape that covered the entrance told the story. With every flashing light of the ambulance, every hope of a miracle was gone. Alan's body had already been removed, the needle still in his arm. The coroner on scene confirmed her worst fears.

Slowly but surely, Alan's family began to heal. His mom was emotionally crushed, and it was obvious that at firstshe was powerless over her grief. However, instead of burying herself under the weight of sorrow and loss, she began to ask what her new role would be in the fight against heroin addiction.

Alan's mother knew that the anger toward drugs and the toll it had taken on Alan and her family had to be used in a positive manner. She began looking for answers that would hopefully save lives and prevent other families from experiencing what she and her family had endured.

Alan's mother, Wendy McCready, wanted a sign from God, a sign that would tell her she was on the right path. She attended many events with other families who had lost children to addiction. During one such event, Wendy talked with a couple that had lost a child to addiction as well. Oddly enough, the husband had been

Alan's roommate at Teen Challenge. He went on to recover and had become a counselor at Teen Challenge.

Wendy shared with them that she was constantly looking for a sign from God that Alan was safe in his arms. A sign would be such a relief. Her wish was about to come true.

It was a beautiful, sunny day. The same couple was standing around Wendy's table as she distributed information about resources available for addiction recovery. It was one of those days when you could feel the glow of the sun and it lifted everyone's spirits. The energy and positive karma coming from everyone attending this event was amazing. The presence of the God of the universe was in the air and it circulated about.

Wendy felt a sudden rush of adrenaline and heard a voice speak to her. The voice told her to look up at the sky. She did, and to the amazement of Wendy and her friend's there was a beautiful rainbow in the clear blue sky. There hadn't been rain in the area for days and there was no scientific reason for a rainbow to be present. Wendy had received the sign that she had so badly wanted. And, as often happens, the sign came out of a clear blue sky.

Today Wendy is involved in many projects, with more to come. She is the founder of "Fight the Fight," a local group dedicated to raising awareness about addiction. They conduct an annual event that raises funds and awareness. Her group provides NARCAN training and free Narcan kits to all who take the training. Her organization helps get people into sober living houses. Wendy is currently working on a sober living house to be named "Alan's House." She and the members of her group attend and support other recovery-oriented events in their community. They attend town hall meetings and interact with education officials, law enforcement members, and policymakers in their town.

Unfortunately, new families are being thrown into this nightmare every day. Wendy and her group of dedicated volunteers are also there to help and comfort those who have suffered a loss due to addiction.

Wendy McCready got off the bench of a victim, a tear in her eye and her teeth clenched with determination. She stepped up to the plate of a parent's worst fear. She swung at the ball and hit it out of the park. It landed in a field of awareness and education for her community. Wendy once felt powerless over her grief; now her dedication and hope empower her.

Wendy McCready is as kind as she is committed. She is an "All-Star" of addiction awareness.

Look back into Wendy's story and consider how any 12-step program could be used to help you, no matter how difficult things seem.

In the beginning, Wendy felt powerless over her grief. This was a grief so powerful, it made parts of Wendy's life unmanageable.

Wendy came to believe that a power greater than herself could restore her.

Wendy made a decision to turn her life and her loss over to the care of the God of her understanding.

Wendy sought relief through prayer and meditation. She turned her grief into something positive.

As a result of these steps, Wendy is able to give back to her community.

Wendy is active in recovering from her grief. She knows that the only way to get through such a tragedy is to become part of the solution. She takes action and by doing that she can maintain a life of service to others.

UNBEARABLE GRIEF

The previous writings described three different families who lost a child to addiction. The stories depicted a shift in their thinking. Instead of accepting their unbearable grief as a permanent condition, they took personal action.

If you or someone you know has suffered the loss of a loved one, help is available. These losses can be so painful that some people will isolate themselves from family members, friends, and people in general.

Some of these family members were mad at God and asked, "If there is a God, how could he do this to me or let something like this happen?" Others feel horribly guilty because they couldn't remedy the situation, or they think they could have done more. This next one is perhaps the hardest; they feel guilty because they experience a sense of relief that the situation is finally over.

The twelve steps of any recovery program can help those who suffer. You can utilize these steps by fitting them into your circumstances.

Step one of any recovery program states; Admit that you have become powerless over something and as a result of that your life has become unmanageable. If you feel powerless over your grief and it is causing you to do things that you wouldn't normally do, your life may have become unmanageable.

Step two of most recovery programs states that you must come to believe that a power greater than yourself can relieve this suffering and restore your life back to normal. For many people this power greater than themselves is a God of their understanding. If this does not work for you, could the knowledge of a group of people who are winning their battle over their grief be a power greater than yourself? There are groups that meet and share how they are working on recovering from their grief. I would suggest finding a local group if possible. There are many social media groups that talk about the loss of a loved one. However, actual interaction with other people has worked best for many.

A good way to start is to say the words out loud: "I am powerless over my grief and my life has become unmanageable." When an alcoholic admits that they are powerless over alcohol, they open the door to recovery. When you admit that you are powerless over your grief, the door to healing swings open.

You can search for a copy of any 12-step recovery program online. I would suggest reading all 12 steps. In the case of unbearable grief not all of the 12-steps will seem to apply to you. However, if you print a copy and keep it handy, you will be amazed by how many of the steps can help you.

Once you admit that you are powerless over your grief your mind will start searching for an answer. Like the recovering alcoholic you will see results and you will begin to believe that grief recovery is possible.

Your recovery will open doors in your life that seemed impossible to open and you will heal. Become the type of person who is interested in full recovery and helping others. Sharing how you overcame your once unmanageable grief will help others. You know their pain and you can make a difference.

Using a twelve-step program is only one way to learn to overcome grief. Search for others and never give up.

NOTE FROM A FRIEND

When I asked a dear friend how she was able to move on with her life after losing her young husband to cancer I was enlightened and inspired to share her thoughts.

I was raised on a farm. I was taught to get up, get dressed, and put one foot in front of the other. You did what you had to do to get done what needed to get done. There was never any thought of waiting until tomorrow to address anything.

This is how I must deal with my grief. I have to get up everyday and put one foot in front of the other, then, do my best.

CHAPTER TWO

THE VICTIMS

THE STORM STARTED IN HIS MIND

Rage comes upon a person instantly. There is no distinct line that's recognizable, it migrates from anger to rage in a flash. There is a feeling of blackness and a numb sensation. Many people who have experienced rage describe it as a blank feeling. All a person see's in their mind is an empty space that's dark and feels like fire. That feeling of numb and burn migrates to the person's core infecting their entire body. This gives it permission to use all its powers to inflict the most damage possible without any thought of the consequences. Anger is an emotion, its part of all of us. Angry feelings are as normal as happy feelings. A fit of rage is an action.

MJ is the victim and the survivor in this story.

One night, MJ and her husband were entertaining some close friends. They all were having fun and listening to music. MJ had been dancing with her friend's husband and all seemed to be enjoying the evening. Dark storm clouds began to churn in MJ's husband's jealous and drunken mind. The storm in his mind waited patiently for their friends to leave. His cold stare shifted when his wife asked him "what's wrong?"

With that, the storm hit with all its might and with a deluge of furious rain. In front of their eight year- old daughter, MJ's husband pinned MJ's arms down with his knees and released the hurricane. He pounded her in the face with his fists never hearing their daughter begging for him to stop. Maybe he didn't hear her cries because all through the bludgeoning he was screaming his ex-wife's name. Part of his rage apparently was attached to his first failed marriage. Perhaps he had realized the fact that his first wife had caught on to his sick way of thinking and that had haunted him for years. Like all storms, they eventually run out of power, and it was not until he was exhausted did the rain stop falling.

After ten years of marriage, his "crazy" had finally surfaced. His alcoholism had reached a new level and his alcoholic narcissism appeared in the sunlight for all to see.

Having grown up in a beautiful and loving home, MJ had never experienced someone having power over her or her thinking. When MJ occasionally questioned why her husband was doing something a certain way with regards to their money, he would immediately show signs of anger. He then would turn off his outward appearance of being angry like a light switch. This made it easier for him to manipulate her into agreeing with him. It was textbook gaslighting.

Gaslighting is defined as such. It is abusive behavior, specifically when the abuser manipulates information in such a way that it causes the victim to begin to question themselves or even their sanity.

The results of this on a regular basis will cause the victim to be dumbed down so to speak. In other words, the victim will stop questioning the abuser's decisions in order to avoid conflict.

Being married to a manipulative alcoholic came with a price for MJ. The lies and the constant burden of tiptoeing around his mood swings was exhausting. She was being broken down a fragment at a time and tiny pieces of herself was being torn from her. he constant abuse becomes their normal. Her own dreams were stripped away from her without mercy, her inner pain was excruciating.

It was during this time periods that MJ became pregnant. The doctor announced that MJ was pregnant with Triplets! MJ was elated and could not wait to make the big announcement to her husband. Her husband did not share in her excitement. He screamed, "How are we going to be able to pay for all this? Who is going to take care of all these kids, and how are we going to raise all these children?"

Slowly but surely, he began to try to convince her to abort these children. At first, MJ would have none of it. She purchased three cribs, clothes, and a variety of other things necessary to bring home their babies. With every purchase, she was chastised. "Look how much this is costing already" was one of her husband's common statements. Almost every time he noticed MJ relaxing, he would seize that opportunity to grind on her conscience. "You need to start thinking about everything we are going to be giving up when those kids get here, he would remark." There never seemed to be a time for MJ to distance herself from him and his never-ending verbal abuse.

The constant verbal abuse, along with the never-ending gaslighting started to wear MJ down. Her husband was patient because he had used these tactics before to get what he wanted. The feeling of being overwhelmed began to slip into MJ's soul.

MJ needs the world to know that she didn't want to abort her children, but she did. Now, all these years later it still feels like she is dragging around a steel box filled with shame. The weight of shame is unmeasurable.

The marriage became intolerable as a result of his continued verbal, physical, and mental abuse. When it was all said and done, they lost their home to foreclosure, and they lost their marriage due to his unbearable alcoholism.

Near the end, some of MJ's friends suggested to MJ that she consider going to some Al-Anon meetings. These meetings are designed to give comfort to the loved ones of addicted people. They are designed to bring hope and to teach how to set boundaries in the lives of people that are affected by a loved one who is alcoholic.

MJ could not forget the night of her beating in front of their daughter, it seemed to haunt her. It was not until years later that MJ knew she was suffering from PTSD.

PTSD, Post Traumatic Stress Disorder is defined by but not limited to, a mental health condition that's triggered by a terrifying event, either experiencing it or witnessing it.

MJ decided not to attend these meetings. Instead, she chose to read the Big Book of Alcoholics Anonymous. The Big Book teaches how to use a twelve program in alcoholism recovery and how to live without alcohol in a person's life. We, of course, have shared how to use some of these steps of recovery for many different afflictions.

MJ used the twelve steps to recognize some things in her life.

MJ realized and admitted that her life had become unmanageable and that she could not fix it on her own.

MJ came to believe that a power greater than herself could bring peace back into her life. MJ calls her higher power God.

MJ made a fearless and searched moral inventory of herself. This helps us all to recognize our part in the issue.

MJ humbly asked God to help her through her trails.

MJ has recently had an epiphany, and step twelve has begone to sparkle and shine its truth in her life. Step twelve speaks of sharing your strength and hope with others. She has now reached out to help others who are still suffering from similar traumas in their lives. MJ is now giving back to her community and with using her social media influence to reach out to others. She wants to share her story of abuse. She wants to share her story of having an unwanted abortion just to give into someone else's demands.

MJ is beginning to see the promises of AA come true in her life. She is starting to know a new freedom and a new happiness. MJ still works closely with her therapist. MJ is a hero in my eyes, and I hope your eyes as well. She has come forward and told her story with no agenda other than to give back to the world. Someone who is as courageous as MJ is will realize that this is just a start, her possibilities are endless.

I'M JUST A GIRL

Fee-B was walking down the street to meet her next customer when she heard tires squeal. She looked up in time to see three men jump from their still-running van. In an instant, they had her. They threw her into the van and taped her legs, arms, and mouth. Terrified, Fee-B couldn't imagine what she was about to endure and the rage that would remain with her for years to come.

At the age of two or three, Fee-B was drinking the leftover swill at the bottom of her alcoholic parents' beer cans. The actions were encouraged by her parents and their friends. Fee-B liked the "funny feeling" she got when she drank alcohol. She said, "When all you know is alcoholic dysfunction then it feels normal. I saw my mother and all the women around me treated like dirt and I thought that's the way it is supposed to be."

At age nine, she was raped by a trusted neighbor. The rapist, in his 20s, penetrated a nine-year-old child's body. When she told everyone in the family what had happened, no one believed her. Why would they? She was just a girl.

She thought it was perfectly normal that her dad would take her two older brothers with him when her parents divorced. Although it hurt, she remembers thinking, 'I'm a girl and he doesn't want me anyway.'

She thought that was how life was when her mother moved her and her two younger brothers into the filth of a cockroach-infested motel room. Fee-B thought that Slim Jim's and soda from the bar where her mother worked constituted a normal family supper. She witnessed first-hand how she felt a woman should be treated. She didn't know anything else.

Fee-B went out on her own at the age of 16. She met a boy she thought was going to be the love of her life, but it didn't end up that way. Fee-B dated this young man off and on and stayed with her mother off and on. Fee-B's mother told her that this man was no good, but Fee-B wouldn't listen. Fee-B's mother hadn't exactly been a positive role model when it came to choosing men, so Fee-B ignored her.

At this point, Fee-B and her boyfriend were doing an assortment of illegal drugs. They took or used anything they could get their hands on. Fee-B learned how to feed her and her boyfriend's habit by selling drugs for a local dealer. That kept them high, and her boyfriend was all for it. They were literally living in a hole in the wall of a building located in a filthy alley. It was dark and stank, but it kept the weather off them.

Fee-B became pregnant and gave birth to a baby boy. She was on food assistance as well as the WIC program for new mothers. As fast as she brought home food, her boyfriend ate it all, including the baby food. Fee-B and her baby went to bed hungry more than once.

Fee-B was still pushing drugs and keeping them both high. She did what she had to do to keep the baby from going hungry and away from her boyfriend. However, it was obvious that the child was in imminent danger.

When their son was nine months old, Fee-B did what would be unthinkable to most mothers. She gave her son to her sister and told her to keep him. As heartbreaking as it was, Fee-B knew it would be the best thing to do.

Fee-B went back to work hustling and selling drugs for money to keep both herself and her boyfriend high. At this point, they were addicted to heroin and cocaine. One morning Fee-B couldn't wake up her boyfriend. He wasn't dead, but he just pushed her away and remained sleeping in their little hole.

While Fee-B was gone, her boyfriend woke up and tried to shoot up his last bit of heroin, but he fell back to sleep. While he was asleep, the heroin dried up. When he awoke, he was out of heroin and was furious.

Fee-B returned home loaded with dope and money, before she could say anything, her boyfriend attacked her in a fit of rage. He pushed her off the 10-foot loading dock that was part of their roof. With a loud thud, Fee-B fell into the alley face first and was seriously injured. In an instant, she regained her wits and ran for it. She ran out of the alley and, to her surprise, right into several guys who liked her and were her customers.

Fee-B's boyfriend was right behind her. Within a few minutes, it seemed like 10 guys were pounding and stomping him. Fee-B never went back.

When word of what had happened got back to Fee-B's dealer, he was enraged. He somehow found her and took her to a motel. She was safe and warm and laid up for a few days nursing her wounds. She would never return to her boyfriend or that hideous alley.

Back on the streets, Fee-B was doing ok. She reached out to her mother, still seeking her acceptance. Fee-B's mother wanted Fee-B back in her life but only if Fee-B would stop doing drugs and only drink alcohol. Fee-B put down the drugs and grabbed ahold of the bottle. She spent the next three years drunk and pregnant. Fee-B had met a good man whom she would later marry. They moved in together and had two children.

As dysfunctional as all this was, it was the closest thing to normal that Fee-B had ever known. However, it was short-lived. One day, when her man was at work, their neighbor offered Fee-B a bit of heroin. That was all she needed; Fee-B was off chasing the white dragon once again.

Fee-B remarked, "I'm not like a normal addict who comes home at night. I disappear for days, sometimes weeks." The whole family was in an uproar as Fee-B gave in to her addiction. Fee-B was lost and wandering.

Fee-B's husband took their children to Mexico to stay with his family. His family in Mexico was doing their best to accept Fee-B, but she was always causing a scene.

Fee-B became ill one night, and her husband thought she had gotten some bad dope. However, that wasn't the case. Fee-B spent the next six months in the hospital with a bacterial infection caused by drinking water in Mexico.

After the initial shock of the situation eased up, Fee-B was back at it. Her associates started bringing her heroin in the hospital. She used daily, hiding her syringe in a plant they had brought her. Fee-B openly admitted, at that point in her life, she would do anything to get high, even if it meant trying to stick her needle into her IV.

When Fee-B was released from the hospital, she didn't go home. Instead, she found a hotel room and set herself up to start dealing again. As always, Fee-B was successful at keeping herself high and making money for herself and her dealer.

Fee-B didn't go unnoticed by the neighboring dealers. She had popped up out of nowhere and was now stealing their customers. Fee-B was a threat to their livelihood, and they were tired of it. Three men in a van had been watching and plotting Fee-B's demise. Their solution was simple: They were going to remove their problem and make sure it didn't return.

Once she was in the van, Fee-B's eyes darted about in terror. The men didn't bother to hide their faces, and Fee-B knew what that meant. The van pulled into a predetermined abandoned warehouse. The men kicked her out and tied her to an old pillar.

The first day, they tortured her at their leisure. They burned her with a blow torch. They watched her wriggle and flop about with every strike of their flame. Methodically, they raped her, one after another. The horror she tried to emit was lost within herself, as her taped mouth wouldn't allow for more than a muffled noise. With every stifled moan, the rapist seemed to be encouraged instead of remorseful.

After they raped Fee-B, they began to burn her again, this time with cigarettes, using her body as an ashtray. There was no hurry because she wasn't going anywhere. No one on earth—including Fee-B—knew where she was.

As they got ready to leave for the day, one of the men turned around and came back. He wasn't quite done. He pulled out his knife and showed it to Fee-B. He got the response of terror in her eyes that he had hoped for. With that, he stabbed her twice in her side, leaving her wounded and bleeding. Fee-B doesn't think she fell asleep that night; she believes she blacked out from the nightmare of what she had endured.

The next morning, the men arrived back at the warehouse. They spent most of the morning burning her and opening up her wounds from the day before. Fee-B was in and out of consciousness for most of that second day. She would wake up sometimes seeing them, sometimes not. She has no idea how many times she was raped, burned, and urinated on that second day. Fee-B knows one thing for sure, though; she heard them leave and she heard one of them say, "Let's be done with this tomorrow."

On the third and final day, the men returned and picked up where they had left off. They punched, kicked, and burned her some more. During this last round of beatings, Fee-B's body began to writhe uncontrollably; it could stand no more. The men assumed she was dying, and that these were her death moans. Satisfied with their actions, the men started to leave, but then one of them pulled his gun and shot at Fee-B's twisting body, hitting her in the leg and causing her to surge even more. She doesn't remember them leaving. They were gone, having left her for dead.

Fee-B began to come around and regain her wits. She managed to free her hands and legs. Fee-B crawled toward a ray of sunlight in the warehouse. As she got closer, the sunlight grew bigger, exposing the fact that it was an open door. She felt a glimmer of hope when she saw a car go by. Naked and severely wounded, she rolled into the sunlight and onto the sidewalk.

Fee-B calls it a "God Shot" because, unbelievably, the first car to drive by was that of the drug dealer for whom she was working. He jumped out of the car with a blanket and covered Fee-B's trembling body.

Once in the car, her dealer begged Fee-B to let him take her to the hospital. She begged him not to. Fee-B knew that if it came out that she was still alive, her killers would return to murder her.

Her dealer took her to his apartment and began to nurse her back to health. Fee-B was lucky that the knife wounds had missed her lungs and that the gunshot had passed through the fleshy part of her thigh. It took a couple of months for Fee-B to recover from her physical injuries, but it took years to recover from the trauma of it all.

After the kidnapping and murder attempt, Fee-B couldn't cope with her life. She didn't want to feel anything, and she didn't want to be touched. Fee-B went back on the streets, selling drugs and staying drunk and high. She became vicious. She got a gun and committed multiple armed robberies against other dealers and the people living on the streets. Fee-B admits, "I would stick a gun to someone's head in a heartbeat. I didn't care if I lived or died." Years later, a therapist would tell Fee-B that role reversal is common among those who have been brutalized. When Fee-B was using her gun to strike terror into one of her victims, she was seeking some sort of power over them—a power that she had been denied during her ordeal.

Fee-B spent the next 10 years on the streets, in and out of jail, sleeping in a tent or wherever she could lay down. She stayed in contact with her ex-husband, but only to get money from him. She wasn't in contact with any other family members during this period. One day when she met her ex-husband, he brought along their daughter, whom Fee-B hadn't seen in 10 years. Her daughter pleaded with her to get help and told her that her son wanted to talk to her as well.

Fee-B didn't really care. What she was interested in was getting the money from her ex and getting high. Fee-B did give her daughter a phone number where she could be contacted, and the next day her son called her. That conversation altered Fee-B's life forever.

When Fee-B asked about her mother, her son told her that her mother had died three years earlier and that her father had died only a few months earlier. Fee-B dropped to her knees and screamed for God to help her. It was a genuine prayer for God to intervene in her life. God answered by sending a friend whom

Fee-B hadn't seen in a long time. The friend arrived at Fee-B's door at five o'clock the following morning. So began Fee-B's journey to a life of addiction recovery.

Fee-B's friend took Fee-B to a detox center. For the next 11 days, Fee-B's physical body was in a state of living hell. Purging the toxins from her system was horrific. Her body convulsed daily, and every muscle contorted constantly. Fee-B was already very thin but by the end of 11 days, she had lost an additional 17 pounds.

After detox, Fee-B went to several long-term recovery programs. Spending six months clean in an inpatient facility was her start. Sober living houses followed. Fee-B had detoxed from the drugs in her system, but not from the life she had lived for so many years. She wore her rage on her sleeve for all the world to feel at the slightest provocation.

After two years of being clean and sober, Fee-B lived a life that was far from peace-filled or content. She was living in a sober living room on Skid Row in Los Angeles, surrounded by dysfunction of every variety. She was miserable and began thinking that if this was what sobriety was, she'd be better off high.

One bright and warm morning, Fee-B walked out of her room and onto the crowded street. She had a deeper feeling of hopelessness than usual and had just about given up. She asked God why should she even try.

Just then, a booming voice entered Fee-B's mind. It said, "This could be you!" It was so real and so loud, she couldn't ignore it. She looked around and saw a crackhead lying on the sidewalk. The voice screamed, "This could be you!" She looked a little farther, where someone else was being loaded into an ambulance. Someone was shooting up heroin right next to her. A guy was smoking crack. All around her, people were miserable and begging for money or food. "This could be you!" the voice of God repeated over and over in her mind. At that moment, Fee-B had a rare and humbling feeling in her soul. That feeling was gratitude, and it changed her life.

Today, over seven years later, Fee-B is still clean and sober. Her children are in her life and she is a grandmother. Fee-B regularly attends NA meetings and has a sponsor who holds her accountable. She sponsors newcomers in the NA program, teaching them the steps that saved her life. She uses the 12 steps of NA in every area of her life and has turned her life over to the God of her understanding. Fee-B has made a great effort to use the 12 steps of recovery in her everyday life and she is winning.

Over the years of addiction, Fee-B's teeth had rotted away. She was embarrassed and covered her mouth when she talked to someone. Today, she has new teeth and proudly shows off her smile when she exclaims, "God gave me my smile back." Most days, Fee-B is smiling.

Like Fee-B's smile, her story gleams with hope and with what is possible for everyone who seeks victory over their struggles.

THE EMPTY BOX

Unfortunately, domestic violence can go hand in hand with alcoholism and drug addiction. Our story about CH depicts the worst of both.

Murder never entered her mind and why should it. Her father's regular beatings of her mother didn't equate to murder. After she had attended a school function with her brother, they returned home to see police cars in their driveway. CH's father was arrested for conspiracy to commit murder for hire.

CH's alcoholic father's plan for murder by hire had backfired. Her father had made an "arrangement" the night before the murder was to be executed. He had decided that his wife had to go. His murderous mind drew a complete diagram of their home under the watchful eye of the would-be assassin. The diagram showed various entry points around the house along with the pros and cons of using each one. The victim's arrival and departure times were noted, as well as prime opportunities to enter, kill, and then flee with the least resistance. The drunken mastermind had it all figured out. Now the thing that was causing all his problems would be eliminated, his wife.

The potential killer had agreed to the terms, but the whiskey had skewed his judgment. Once sober, he immediately went to the police and disclosed his former employer's plot. CH's father was arrested but not prosecuted. Her father had somehow wormed his way out of jail time.

Straight out of high school, CH joined the military. There she met a man whom she would eventually marry. At CH's young age, she was surrounded by people who were older than she was, making alcohol readily available. CH recognized that if she continued the path of using alcohol, she would eventually turn into an alcoholic like her father. With that in mind, she was very cautious regarding her drinking and didn't drink often.

With that steadfastness in her mind, CH readily accepted an invitation to a casual party. Her drinking started out innocently but progressed quickly. One of the last things she can remember is going to the bathroom to throw up. She knows she came back and sat on the couch. The next time she woke up, she was naked on the floor with someone on top of her. He was actively raping her, and she recognized him. Her consciousness was brief, and she passed out again. The next time she woke up, she was still being raped, but by a different guy. Once again, she lost consciousness.

CH firmly believes she continued to pass out as a defense mechanism. The reality of what was happening to her was too much for her conscious mind to endure. The next reality that came to her was that she was fully dressed and being carried to the car by her assailants. CH knew full well who they were. They lived in the same barracks that she did. When asked if she had reported this incident to her superiors, she said she never had because of the shame she felt.

Her shame was undeserved. The damage that the rapists had done was far from over. CH began to drink heavily. Hidden in her room, she drank alone in the dark.

CH's husband was stationed in Germany. He was in Iraq at the time but was due back in Germany, so CH moved to Germany. She was out of the military and living by herself, awaiting his return. Her habit of drinking everyday continued.

Upon his return, CH realized that he had changed. She recognized that the things he'd done and seen while in Iraq had completely changed him. She also realized that the fallout from her rape had changed her as well. What had once been a wonderful relationship was over; they had become two different people. Like so many others, her fear of reporting her attack prevented her mind from healing. Her physical discomfort had long gone. But her shame would leave a wound open for years.

CH returned home. Back in the States, her drinking escalated even further. CH couldn't hold a job. Somehow, she put herself through nursing school, drunk every day. She graduated and looked forward to a long and prosperous career.

CH met a man who was a recovering heroin addict, fresh out of prison. They began a relationship that looked wonderful and within a few months, CH became pregnant. Although their relationship looked good from the outside, they were living a lie. He relapsed time and again. CH recognized that he had to go into treatment and he agreed. Now six months pregnant, CH was forced to move back in with her mother.

Once out of the treatment center, CH's boyfriend moved in with CH and her mom. His time there was brief, he started stealing her mother's pain pills and was forced to leave. He did leave something else behind besides his newborn baby. He left CH with the notion that she could take pain pills with no repercussions. CH knew she liked them too much and tried to stop, but it was too late. Her journey into prescription pain pill addiction had begun.

CH had kept up with her ex-boyfriend. One day, she made a phone call to him that changed her life forever. CH told him she wanted to try heroin and he gladly met her request. CH's first taste of heroin came through her nose. The next day, CH shot up for the first time.

The first few weeks of CH's heroin use didn't seem too bad to her. That changed. She became obsessed with heroin and willingly abandoned her daughter leaving her with her mother. She didn't return to work and she moved in with her man. CH's story was textbook, she had become a heroin addict. She lost weight and became gaunt. Every penny of money she could hustle up went to the dope man.

After months of shooting up every day, CH woke up one morning dope sick and desperate. Dope sick is a heroin high in reverse. The pleasure one feels during the high is equal to pain one suffers during the with-drawl. Miserable, she decided to reach out for help. Help was found and she ended up in a 28-day recovery facility. CH completed the treatment and she felt great. She moved back in with her mother and took care of her daughter. Things were good until they weren't.

After a routine trip to the doctor, CH's mother was diagnosed with stage four cancer. CH was devasted; her best friend in the world was dying. CH's life was going to change forever. CH took care of her mother the best she could, but she didn't deal with the reality of the situation very well. CH began to steal her mother's Oxycontin and, later, her Percocet.

Her mom was weak but coherent. One day she discovered that her pills were being taken. CH's mother decided to put them all in a lockbox with the assumption that they would be safe there. However, CH wouldn't be deterred. She googled the lockbox information and within minutes had it open. Earlier that day, CH had dropped off a prescription for her mother's Percocet. She knew her mother wouldn't be short when she needed them to treat her pain. CH decided, "No harm, no foul" and stole all the Percocet from the box. The events that transpired next would leave a lifelong scar on CH's heart.

CH returned home that day and had an odd feeling. CH began looking around the house for her mother. Finally, she opened the door to the room where the lockbox was stored. There, on the floor, was her mother staring at the empty box.

Her mother looked up at CH and CH could see the pain in her glossy, stained-glass eyes. Her eyes were stained with tears over unrealistic expectations. Her mother's eyes were stained by the overwhelm of it all, her cancer, her daughter's addiction, and every mistake she had ever made in her life.

Real or imagined, CH claims she witnessed a transformation in her mother. Her mother would never have that tiny spark of hope in her eyes again. Within a few short months, her mother lost her battle and was set free at last.

Once her mother's estate was settled, CH received a check for a little over $20,000. She immediately quit her job and got an apartment on her own. CH went on a spree and spent thousands of dollars buying drugs for herself and her friends. CH was out of money before her first rent payment was due.

Daily heroin use was back in CH's life. In a few months, CH called her brother and told him she could no longer raise her daughter in a safe environment. She asked if he could take her in. Her brother accepted the offer and welcomed CH's daughter into his home.

CH was exhausted. She was tired of all the pain and the mayhem in her life. Something had to change, so she signed up at a methadone clinic. Not long after that, CH admitted herself into treatment at a VA hospital. There, she was weaned off the methadone and released. During her stay, she met a guy, and they moved to his hometown. CH and her boyfriend had applied for disability and both received it, along with the back pay. Between them, they received $50,000. It wasn't long before the money was gone and they were down to pawning everything that they had bought with the money. They broke up a couple of times and eventually CH moved back to her hometown.

Shacked up in a flophouse motel, CH was living the life of the damned, sick and addicted. CH had left the motel and ended up at a friend's house. There, one of her long-time friends OD'd but lived. This was the first time CH got scared and realized that this would be her one day. It didn't scare her enough to stop using but the seed of hope had been planted.

This seed of hope grew and took root. One day, CH woke up with one pocket full of money and the other full of painkillers. She was worn down to nothing. Her life didn't work anymore; the stress of the day-to-day struggle had taken its toll on her, both physically and mentally. Enough was enough. She put herself in a treatment center in North Carolina. CH showed a desire to succeed and learned all she could about the 12 steps of addiction recovery and how to live a clean life.

After treatment, her ex-boyfriend contacted her. He wanted her to move away with him again. This time, CH said no. A few months after she saw him, he overdosed and died.

CH is the first to admit that life isn't perfect. There are still deep family problems that are works in progress. Today she is in active recovery. That means she takes steps every day to maintain her sobriety. She has a sponsor and goes to Narcotics Anonymous meetings on a regular basis.

The blessing of her nursing degree has put her in a perfect spot to help others and to give back to a world she once took for granted. CH is a nurse at a Veterans Administration hospital. Her ability to help other vets is a dream come true. CH is living the miracle of recovery.

CH got off the bench of a victim and stepped up to the plate of an organization that helps thousands. She took a mighty swing of her personal miracles and hit a home run into a life that serves many. CH is alive and well, living her dream.

No matter what your circumstances are, there is a 12-step program that you can use to create a plan for success in life. The key is to take action.

WHERE THE ALLIGATORS PLAY

K closed her eyes and covered her ears, hoping it would stop. Her brothers lay terrified in their beds as the screams of the hopeless victim grew louder. They cried and prayed but they were helpless to make the screams go away. When the screams turned to moans, the worst of it had just begun for a child who should have been asleep and dreaming – dreaming of a fairy tale land where all was wonderful instead of arising from her bed to do what she had to do.

K's alcoholic father lay exhausted from having beaten her mother relentlessly. Her mother had crawled to the bathroom and somehow gotten herself in the tub. Her hopes were that the warm water would wash away her pain and maybe a little bit of the memory of what she had just endured.

Now by her side, K tried to ease her mother's agony by gently washing away the blood. Her washcloth was the only tool she had to try to subdue her mother's agony. She instinctively spoke to her mother in soft tones: "It will be ok, I'm here." They were words that a six-year-old should not be speaking to her mother, though the words calmed K as well and felt natural. These are the interior wounds that K still carries. They are still so close under her skin that a tiny scratch opens a flood of unsettled hurts.

K's childhood was filled with mental trauma, dysfunction, and divorce. At nine, she started taking sips of the poison that would dominate her life for years to come. By 11, she was stealing liquor from the family cabinet. By 12, she was huffing gasoline and rubber cement almost daily. Huffing is the act of deliberately inhaling the fumes of toxins, resulting in an immediate high. The high doesn't last very long, so the huffing must be repeated, again and again. K's mother walked into her room unexpectedly one night and saw a mess of rubber cement on her bed with K was passed out next to it. Her mother knew nothing of this activity, so K was able to blow it off with an easy lie.

At age 13, K moved in with her father. When she began ninth grade, K began hanging out with others like herself. She and her friends began using acid and other hard drugs. Smoking dope and drinking had now become a regular part of their lives.

One day, K and her best friend made a run for it. They skipped school and disappeared. The frigid temperatures didn't deter them. They were on the loose and walking from one place to another. They ended up in an area of town that had the biggest drug problem, the highest high school drop-out rate, and the highest percentage of teen pregnancy.

The streets were dirty and reeked of hopelessness. They felt exempt from it all, like they were there but not part of it. These were two very pretty young girls who were welcomed into every known dope house they found. When the dope ran out, they simply walked to the next one. They slept wherever they fell asleep and they stole food, clean underwear, and anything they needed from the local stores. This went on for four days.

At the end of the fourth day, they were walking around, freezing. Out of nowhere, K's father, who had been searching for her, pulled up next to them. K had had enough and willingly jumped in the car. Her friend ran and K's father immediately called her friends parents. K was shaking uncontrollably and couldn't get warm. Concerned, her father rushed her to the ER. Her internal temperature was 89 degrees. The nurses and doctors were shocked that she wasn't in a deadly phase of hypothermia. This condition kills people, but it wasn't K's time.

K's next stop was a center for troubled teens and drug rehabilitation. First, she was given Prozac but her body rejected it. Next, K was given Ritalin, which she quickly learned how to crush into powder form and snort.

Upon release, K was given two full prescriptions for Ritalin. That night, she crushed and snorted both bottles. She couldn't stop her mind from wanting more. She had been on the phone talking with her boyfriend and had told him what she had done. He was concerned but her words weren't slurred and she was talking relatively sanely. He hung up with a bad feeling inside, and it began to slowly haunt his thoughts.

That night, K began picking at her face. She stood in the bathroom mirror and picked her face into a horrible, bloody mess.

The relentless picking of one's face is a behavior common among people who have taken massive amounts of drugs.

K's face appeared to have been picked completely off. Her mother took one look at this horrific sight and began screaming and crying. She begged K to go to the hospital. K refused and went to bed.

Her boyfriend could stand no more of the nagging intuition that wouldn't stop. He called her mother and told her what K had snorted. He told her to get K to the hospital.

Her mother left her no alternative and took K to the ER. K was walking and talking normally. At the check-in desk, she asked where the bathroom was because she felt like she was going to throw up. In the bathroom, she began vomiting green bile. Like a scene from the movie The Exorcist, she vomited so hard it covered the walls and floor. Her mother heard all this and opened the bathroom door. She screamed for help, and the staff got K to a room, where they pumped her stomach. The sight of what was coming from her stomach and into the catch jar stunned and horrified the staff. They had never seen anyone who'd had that much Ritalin in their system and who was still alive. The results of that much Ritalin in someone's system almost always lead to the patient entering a vegetative state and never waking up. K had survived another close call.

K spent a brief period of time in New Mexico. Then she and a couple of friends moved to Florida. K's life would be in danger again. Using Ecstasy, acid, and anything else they could find became their daily routine. Their house became a known party house. Strangers, with all their secrets, drifted in and out with no explanation other than to get high. One of the strangers would alter K's life forever.

The Florida humidity in the summer is debilitating to most people. The foliage grows thick and the swamps are separated only by winding dirt roads that, in the rainy season, disappear completely due to the high water. The roads are rediscovered only during the heat and drought of summer.

The water and plant life sway in the breeze, always in harmony and playing an age-old song. The wildlife slithers across the roads at its leisure, then disappears again into the vastness of the other side. The sounds of the glades are muffled not only by the foliage but by the weight of the air itself. The local small-town gathering places held posters and pictures of the missing, some pictures yellowed by age. To disappear here was to be gone forever, leaving families staring into the abyss of the endless sawgrass, hoping for a return of their loved ones but knowing the truth in their hearts.

It was here where K would learn a harsh life lesson. One of the frequent guests at her party house seemed unassuming and friendly, calm and trustworthy. One day, he approached K with a proposition to make some good money. The stranger claimed that his mother needed in-home care and a house cleaner. K jumped at the chance to make some much-needed money, so they hopped in his car and took off for his mother's. The drive seemed long and the winding dirt roads put them deep into the Everglades. He claimed that his mom lived "way out." It wasn't until he stopped the car deep in the Everglades that K's alarm bells went off. He asked her to open the glove box, saying he had something to show her. When she opened the glove box, K saw the gun. Before she could react, he had it in his hand.

The stranger pressed it firmly to her head and assured her that one of two things was about to happen. Either she would meet his demand for sex or her brains were going to land in the swamp. He then remarked, "Look where you are. You're in the middle of nowhere and no one on this earth knows where you are except me." He assured her that after he blew out her brains, he could easily dispose of her lifeless body. The smell of rotting carrion in the air attracted the giant lizards of the swamp, and he added that the gators weren't picky.

Her terrified mind went into overdrive. "What if I give him sex and he kills me anyway? What's to prevent him from killing me? What if that had been his plan all along?"

She was out of options. K slowly got out of the car and met his rancid demands. Satisfied with his despicable act, and much to her relief, the stranger told her to get in the car so that he could take her home. He reminded her of the consequences of her saying anything to anybody. The threat felt very real and K took an oath of silence. He was never seen again. Years later, K found out that he had done the same thing to one of her roommates, leaving her with the same grim promise of revenge.

A series of events left K lost and deeply depressed. Homeless, hopeless, living by her wits, and working odd jobs to get by became her life. K found an apartment only to be evicted for partying too loud and into the early morning hours. K was taken in by a church member only to be asked to leave due to her reckless behavior.

Change was in the air and K began trying to find a God of her understanding. Finally, enough was enough and K's mother helped her get back to Michigan. Her mom helped her get an apartment. It was in the same bad area where K and her friend had taken their four-day runaway journey. However, there was only so much money available for renting a place and that's what they could afford. The crime rate hadn't changed, and soon K's apartment was broken into and a thief had stolen everything K owned.

Her long run of bad decisions had taken its toll on K. She was jailed for drunk driving; her kids coming to visit her in jail was the beginning of the end. K had sworn to never put her children through the same hell her parents had put her through. However, as with so many others, it had become her reality. The guilt and shame of her actions began viciously attacking K's brain. The endless loops of self-hatred ran non-stop in her mind. She was paralyzed by fear and imprisoned by her thoughts.

At this point, K realized that something had to give; she could no longer stand the brutal pain of a life led astray and a lifetime of addiction.

K now states, "I was living in one specific frequency in the universe, not realizing there is a whole spectrum available to me."

K began running the gamut of addiction recovery resources, including AA. Although she was still using, the progression of her recovery was taking form and becoming a presence in her life.

In 2013, on a whim, K saw a psychic at the county fair. She was broken down both physically and mentally. The psychic told K that her energies were out of balance, which was why she was what she was. K was also told that she had a very dark aura. When she asked where this darkness was coming from, the psychic told her, "It's coming from you."

K had a breakthrough and began researching Reiki spiritual healing. Things and people began appearing in her dreams. Her mind opened and light began to shine in. She went to her first Reiki healing session and felt amazing. Her eyes were wide open and she became hungry for more. After K's first session, her drug use stopped completely. She has remained drug-free to this day. K's drinking lingered for a while longer but left her without incident and she remains sober today.

This woman's story is amazing. K now lives a life of sobriety and has restored her family. There are those who will be skeptical of her beliefs and methods. Know this respect all of God's world and seek the freedom of the universe; you will live a happier and longer life. That is a motto by which K lives every day.

K's story is filled with opportunities for her to apply the 12 steps of Alcoholics Anonymous. She is living its promises. It all revolves around her seeking and finding a power greater than herself. K came to believe that a power greater than herself could restore her to sanity … and it did.

Today, K is dedicated to her practice and to helping others gain spiritual clarity.

THE PAST-LET GO TO GROW

In the previous three stories, you have read about people who suffered from domestic violence and rape. Although their stories are different one thing remains the same their lives have been altered forever. There will always be a scar from the brutality they have endured.

Some of these people have sought professional help and have learned how to deal with their scars. They have learned that they cannot live a full and productive life as a victim. These people went from victim to survivor to victor. They have found a way to move on with their lives.

There is no one size fits all answer to this kind of trauma. I cannot speak on a professional level about these issues. I can share with you what I have learned about these types of traumatic events.

I have learned that when people stay focused on the event, they are still giving their attacker all the power. The perpetrator has done their damage and in some cases years ago. Therefore, if the victim is still letting the event control their lives, they are still giving their attacker power over them. At the time of the event, they were powerless to stop it. Now, years later they do not have to live with the feelings of powerlessness. There is help available.

Think about it this way to start. Imagine you have a scab on your arm that you continuously pick at it. It seems to take forever to heal, and it leaves a bigger scar. The same is true about peoples past. When people give their painful memories power over them, they are picking open an old scar. If they continue to do this, the scar may never heal and will cause them constant pain. It becomes a vicious cycle. They are all right for a while then something will reopen this old wound causing it to retake control of them.

I would urge everyone who has old unhealed scars to seek counsel. These events can ruin your life. They can steal your destiny.

The people in these stories have taken control of their lives. Be encouraged that you can too. Seek professional counsel. Find a twelve-step program and put it to work for you. The people in these stories are living examples of what is possible. They have all been traumatized yet they have found a way to live free of their old wounds. They are committed to being of service to their community by sharing their strength and hope. Live your life in the solution. When you do, you will quickly see that you will no longer be a victim but, in fact, a victor.

CHAPTER THREE

THEY OUGHT TO PUT IT IN THE WATER

PART ONE

HOW TO STEP INTO FREEDOM

The most amazing thing that I have experienced was when I worked a twelve-step program to stop drinking alcohol. I was also amazed that that I had a vision for this book in the middle of the night and that I had already been using the twelve-steps in different areas of my life. It was an awakening, and it led to these truths about twelve-step programs in general.

The twelve-step method of changing a behavior, a habit, or an addiction has worked for thousands, and it can work for you. Most twelve-step programs have similar steps. The key to success is to incorporate your issue within the steps.

Use the internet to search for twelve-step recovery programs. There are many available that you can use if you shift the words to fit your circumstances.

Step one of most twelve-step recovery programs ask you to admit that you are powerless over something and because of it that part of your life has become unmanageable. For example; If you are an overeater who wants to change your eating habits you must admit that you are powerless over your eating habits. Then acknowledge that because of it this part of your life has become unmanageable.

Step two asks you to come to believe that a power greater than yourself could restore this part of your life to normalcy. For many people, this power greater than themselves is the God of their understanding. If that doesn't work for you, could a power greater

58

than yourself be a group of people who are winning their battle over whatever it is that is negatively affecting their lives? In the case of overeating could that be a group called Overeaters Anonymous?

Step three asks you to make a decision to turn your will and your life over to the God of your understanding. For some it may be a group or a program where the people involved are succeeding in making the changes they desire in their lives.

Step four asks you to make a searching and fearless moral inventory of yourself. This means its time to get honest with yourself. If you want to defeat whatever it is that's holding you back, you will have to be honest with yourself. You will have to ask yourself honest and tough questions if you want to succeed.

Step five asks you to admit to your higher power, to yourself, and to another human being the exact nature of your wrongs. Once you have admitted to your higher power and to yourself the exact nature of your wrongs, admit to a loved one, a close friend, or someone else that you can trust the exact nature of your wrongs. Although this may hurt, this step is vital in your journey.

Step six states that you must be entirely ready to have your higher power remove this particular issue.

Step seven asks you to ask your higher power to remove your shortcomings humbly. Being humble enough to ask for help is imperative. If you are the type of person who thinks you can fix your issue on your own, then more power to you. I didn't change anything in my life until I gave up on trying to fix it on my own. By becoming a humble person, life has opened many doors for me.

Step eight asks you to make a list of all persons you have harmed and to become willing to make amends to them all. You may say to yourself, "My behavior hasn't harmed anyone but myself." If that is the case, then your list should have just one name on it, yours. Are you willing to become humble enough to commit to yourself that you will change your behavior? More often than not, I have found out that when a person thinks that the only one being affected by their behavior is themselves, they were wrong. Think about it, doesn't your behavior effect everyone around you including your loved ones?

Step nine asks you to make direct amends to such people wherever possible except when to do so would injure them or others. These are not referring to physical injury per se. People can be injured by your words and actions.

Step ten states that you are to take a personal inventory of yourself and when you are wrong promptly admit it. The people who are committed to change stay on top of it. They have become humble, and they no longer fear to admit when they are wrong.

Step eleven of most twelve-step recovery programs asks you to seek a conscious contact with your higher power through prayer and meditation. Pray for his will for you and the ability to carry that out.

Step twelve states that as a result of these step you will have a spiritual awakening. You will try to spread your message of success and to practice these principles in all of your affairs.

LOVE YOURSELF

Learn how kindness and how loving yourself without ego will have a major impact on your life. When you live in these two places your potential is unlimited.

A few weeks ago, a newcomer in addiction recovery approached me and asked how she could start feeling better about herself. The same methods that I shared with her can help anyone who commits to incorporating these methods into their life.

Like so many people living in full-blown addiction, the newcomer had not been a very nice person to be around. She had been mad at the world and her mindset said that all her problems had been created by other people and other things. Are you the type of person who blames your circumstances on something or someone else?

This way of thinking does not attract kindness to anyone's life. People had grown weary of listening to the newcomer's woes; when she approached them, they acted disinterested. Her calls weren't being returned and when she unexpectedly showed up at her "friends'" homes, her knocks at the door went unanswered.

Blame, rage, fear, and the deep-down-inside knowledge that she had created this situation in her life left her numb and devoid of kindness.

As the newcomer started getting clarity in her mind. I explained to her that though she did not have drugs in her system, the drug addict still lived there. Recovery programs not only teach people how to stop using but, just as importantly, teach them how to live a clean and sober life. The newcomer was far from getting to this stage of her recovery. Therefore, I shared with her a few tips that would get her heading in the right direction.

I asked the newcomer, point blank: "When was the last time you thought of anyone besides yourself?" When I asked her this, she thought about it for more than a few seconds. I could see in her eyes that her mind was racing to recall the last time she had intentionally thought of someone else's problems instead of her own. I explained that for her to begin feeling better about herself, she would need to look for, and act on, every available opportunity to extend the simplest of kindnesses.

I told her that she would never live free from anger until she began living a grateful and kindness-filled life. This is so simple, it's amazing that so many people don't realize it. Just be nice. Tell everyone "thank you." If the clerk at the convenience store is wearing a name tag, call them by their name. Take a few seconds to tell them something positive and upbeat. Put out unto the world what you would like to receive and you will be amazed at how your life changes. If the newcomer wanted to improve her life, she would have to do a personal inventory and promptly admit when she missed an opportunity to be kind to someone (step work required).

You are reading a self-help book. You want something to change in your life or you want to find a way to improve yourself. Think of everyone you meet as a gatekeeper who will propel you to the next level of growth in your life. If you treat everyone you meet as a gatekeeper, eventually one of those people will be the gatekeeper who allows you to grow to the next level of personal success.

When you think less about yourself and more about others, your life will change. You will become the person whom everyone aspires to be like. You will draw into your life all the right gatekeepers and doors will open to you seemingly out of nowhere. You will form a new and positive habit that you don't even think about.

Look at what this habit can do for you. If you are willing, keep track, for just one day, of every time someone is kind to you. I would be willing to bet that you immediately responded to them with kindness. Did responding with kindness feel better to you than receiving the kindness? You bet it did. You have just deepened your feeling of love for yourself without ego.

One of the most common things I hear is, "I don't know how to forgive myself. Therefore, I don't like myself." The key to forgiving yourself is to be more kind to others.

When this love for yourself is reaffirmed day after day, imagine the type of vibe you are sending out to those who care about you. You will send this vibration of self-love to your kids, spouse, friends, etc. They will start feeling more self-love for themselves and you will receive more of the same in return.

If you now realize that this way of thinking can and will change your life for the better, you should be willing to practice this principle in everything you do. Are you willing to carry this message to others, for example, your kids or grandkids?

If you do this, the promises of any recovery program will tell you that your self-seeking and selfish ways will slip away and that you will know a new freedom and a new happiness. I try to practice these principles in all of my affairs and look at whom I have attracted into my life: you.

#NODRAMA

If your life is filled with constant drama you will never live your life to its fullest potential. You have a hole in your life that will never be filled. There will never be enough drama in your life to satisfy you. You will continue to create more and more drama that will create more and more problems in your life. If you would like to stop this behavior there is an answer in a twelve-step addiction recovery program.

If you are reading this perhaps you have become addicted to drama. You may have become cross addicted. You are addicted to drama and you are addicted to your phone. If your need for constant drama in your life continually creates problems, then you have a problem. If you are using your phone as your main avenue to communicate with others, then you may have a problem.

Obviously, your phone is a communication device that is very important. Most people use their phone in a responsible way for work or interactions with family, friends, etc. I am referring to the type of communication that has replaced personal interactions.

The lack of personally interacting with your community, friends, or co-workers creates a feeling of isolation and a distance between you and real people. For some it has created false courage. Unfortunately, some may type things on their phone that they would never say to someone in person. The opportunity to create a false self-esteem can create havoc in a person's life.

At one point in time, drama took place among, family members, at the office, and among friends. Today one of the top formats people create drama on is on various social media sites.

These type sites offer twenty-four-hour a day availability. Some people have become addicted to the attention they receive by posting and responding on these social media sites. They will spend hours getting involved with any topic and are continuously looking for an opportunity to respond. They will post multiple post at all hours of the day seeking attention. A question you could ask yourself is, "Are my post filled with intention or are they meant to get attention?" There are wonderful social media post that are heartfelt and soulful. They are the type of post that are real and designed to nurture, sooth, and evoke good things. The drama addicted posters try to draw attention to themselves and to promote controversy.

Some people will seek and invite open arguments on line. Some of that will lead to name calling, bullying, or to continual harassment. This has become a way of life for many. Because of that, they have become numb to the fact that they are hurting people. They will say anything true or untrue as if their words were harmless. They hide behind their computer trying to gain attention.

Have these type post slipped into the fabric of your daily life? If you are one of these people you may want to ask yourself why you do what you do. I have heard excuses that range from my face book post don't hurt anyone, to I'm bored so I play on my phone for hours. Take a hard look at yourself, are you one of these people?

One of the biggest problems in changing this behavior is someone's willingness to admit they have a problem. Has anyone ever accused you of being a drama queen or king? Has this happened more than once? Have you ever sensed they were right? Have you ever tried to stop and could not?

Think about the effects that you have on your children. Some children will grow up thinking that your behavior is normal behavior and in their early teens they will begin to mimic you. Would that be enough to convince you that you need to address this issue?

Step one of many addiction recovery programs states that you need to admit you are powerless over some behavior and that part of your life has become unmanageable. Here is one way to find out if you have a problem. It you see a post that upsets you, can you not respond to that post? Do you post things that you know will stir up controversy? Do you get an adrenaline rush and start typing faster when you are responding to a post you don't like? Do you do this on a daily basis?

Step two states you must come to believe that a power greater than ourselves could restore us to sanity. For many people their power greater than themselves is the God of their understanding. If that doesn't work for you perhaps a power greater than yourself would be the wealth of knowledge that has been accumulated that proves that this behavior has many down falls and has a negative impact on both yourself and others around you.

Step four is the next appropriate step into you living in the solution. It says, made a searching and fearless moral inventory of ourselves. If you are willing to do this, you will immediately feel the results. Write down the things that you do that feeds this addiction. Be truthful and harsh with yourself. Then write down the benefits you will receive when you change this behavior. Now, look at what you have written. You will notice that the benefits far outweigh the cost of your continued negative behavior. The key to this step is to actually feel the pain of continuing your current behavior and then to feel the happiness of changing this behavior as well as the positive impact it will have on your life.

Step five states that you must admit to God, to yourself, and to another human being the exact nature of your wrongs. I would encourage you not to take this step lightly. You know you must admit to yourself you have a problem in order to change. It is vital that you admit to someone else the exact nature of your wrongs. This can be frightening but there are options. If you have a trusted friend admit to them what your issues are and tell that person you are seriously working on doing better. Others could include your minister, your spouse or significant other, your priest, or to a group of people you are also committed to changing their lives. You will feel a great sense of relief when you do this and those feeling will strengthen your resolve.

Steps six and seven can be combined here. Step six states that we were entirely ready to have God remove all these defects of character. Step seven states that we humbly ask him to remove our short comings. They both come down to this, you must humble yourself to accept that you have this problem and without help you cannot remedy it by yourself. It is imperative to let go of your ego. It will become nearly impossible to win your battle with out letting go of your ego.

Step eight states for you to make a list of all persons you have harmed and became willing to make amends to them all. They key word in this step is willing. Are you willing to make a list of these people? Are you willing to make amends to them all?

Step nine states that you must make direct amends to such people where ever possible except when to do so may injure them or others. Do not be afraid of this major step. Address the people close to you and make a sincere apology. Let them know that you are taking measures to stop this part of your life. Use caution. Do not pick open old wounds. If you do that you will be creating drama that's unnecessary and obviously you don't want that. Do not expect tell others how much you have changed and be taken seriously. The best apology in the world comes from others looking at how you have changed, it is much more satisfying to show them.

Step ten states that you must continue to take personal inventory and when you are wrong promptly admitted it. This is how you achieve maximum growth. When you start to slip back-wards you will not act on your thoughts. You will continue this new and wonderful life, and now, with the extra time you have, you can raise yourself to the next level of personal growth.

Step twelve can be simplified in this instance. Now that you have stopped living a life addicted to drama and to your phone, are you willing to help others overcome their struggles? People who are living in the solution need to know that when they become involved in helping others it solidifies their own recovery.

Overcoming something like addiction to drama and your phone is freeing and will make you feel unstoppable. Step your way into freedom.

MONEY

Money is not important until you don't have any. If you are the type of person who cannot control your spending, you will continually have financial problems.

If you have tried to stop overspending and you cannot achieve it, you have a problem. You may want to consult a mental health professional to find out the root of this behavior. I am not a mental health professional; however there are steps in every twelve-step program that can be valuable to you. There are even anonymous groups specifically for shopaholics.

Step one of most twelve-step programs states that you must admit that you are powerless over this part of your life and that your life has become unmanageable because of it. If you cannot stop spending money on things you don't need you are powerless over your ability to control your spending and this part of your life has become unmanageable. To overcome your overspending be honest with yourself and admit you are powerless to control it.

Step two states that you must come to believe that a power greater than yourself could remove this issue in your life. Many people relate this to a God of their understanding. If this doesn't work for you could a power greater than yourself be a group or organization comprised of people who are winning their battle over money?

Step three states that you must make a decision to turn your will and your life over to a God as you understand him. The key element here is turning over your will. You must recognize that your continuous overspending is a result of your self will and that your recovery will be based on relinquishing that will.

Step four states that you must become willing to make a searching and fearless inventory of yourself. In essence, became willing, to be honest with your self and to recognize your flaws.

Step five guides you to become willing to admit to God, to yourself and to another human being the exact nature of your wrongs. Admitting to God your wrongs is self-explanatory for believers. Admitting to yourself and to another human being can be as simple as admitting to yourself what you already know and then sharing this with your spouse or a close friend.

Step six states that you have become entirely ready to have God remove all these defects of character. You're overspending may or may not be a character flaw. Your character is not defined by a bad habit. You have become a person with a spending problem. For those who believe in a God of their understanding, praying for help is their solution. For the others, you must be willing to let go of the thing that's holding you back.

Step nine is the next appropriate step when it applied to overspending. Make direct amends to those your overspending has hurt except to do so would injure them or others. An example of this would be you call for a family meeting. This may be a small meeting of your immediate family and telling them you are sorry for your overspending, and you know that it has hurt them. Do not skip this step if you want to continue to win in your recovery. This open and honest apology has tremendous healing power for you and for them.

Step ten tells you to continue to take personal inventory and when you are wrong promptly admit it. If you have a slip, recognize it immediately and then move forward. Keep yourself in the solution and don't revel in a slip.

Step eleven is for those who believe that their higher power is God. It says to seek through prayer and meditation to improve your conscious contact with God as you understand him. Praying only for knowledge of his will for you and the power to carry that out. That is straight forward for the believers. For the others who struggle you may want to look at this as a quiet time you spend reflecting on the progress you have made and the personal growth that comes with it.

Step twelve speaks of having a spiritual awakening and as a result of these steps we must try to carry your message to others and to practice these principles in all of your affairs. Rejoice in the knowledge that you can now live free from any affliction if you are willing to practice these steps in all of your affairs. Having a spiritual awakening for those who believe that God is their higher power is a result in the work they have done using these steps. Could your awakening lead you to help and guide others who still suffer? For the believers and for the non-believers it is said that you must give your knowledge away to keep it. In essence, it is saying live in the solution and share this good news to the world.

WHAT ARE YOU AFRAID OF?

What you are afraid of is either a normal and healthy fear or a self- created fear that will prevent you from achieving your destiny.

That's a pretty bold statement, but it's very accurate. First, let's get legitimate fears out of the way, so we don't confuse the two. If you are afraid to jump off a 10-story building, that is a normal and healthy fear. If you are afraid to take action on a dream of yours because you are worried about what others will think or you are scared to try something because of fear of failure that's a different matter.

Some people are afraid to start something new in their lives because they think it will be too much work. A lot of alcoholics and drug addicts are dead now because they weren't willing to do the work it takes to recover and build a new and beautiful life. They feared the change, they feared the withdrawal process, they feared that their friends would reject them. They're gone simply because they were afraid.

Are you also afraid to step out of your comfort zone? Are you worried that you will create a new idea and do all this work only to fail and be laughed at? Are you afraid of what your friends will say when they see that you are trying to better yourself? *What will they think or say about me?* You must know the following and keep it in your mind. Water always seeks its own level. When you try to rise above the level with which you and your friends are comfortable, some of those friends will reject you.

But what happens if I lose all my friends?Then what will I do? Well, what happens if you don't, and your friends keep you from achieving your destiny?

All things have a season; there is a reason why these friends are in your life. Some of these people you love, some of these people are your family. I'm not saying to be mean or hateful to these people; it's essential that you love them all. However, if these people aren't helping to propel you toward your future, maybe you should start hanging around with new friends who will.

Once again, water seeks its own level. I want to be completely honest with you. I have friends whom I know in my heart would never believe that I was capable of writing this book...yet here you are reading it. I have tried many ideas. Some succeeded, some didn't. I refuse to avoid trying something I believe has a chance simply because I'm afraid of what my friends might say. It wasn't always that way, but it is now.

Think about it this way: Do you think anyone who achieved long-term sobriety kept the same friends they had when they were using? They changed friends to become successful. Are you willing to do the same?

Stepping outside the box and outside your comfort zone takes courage. Here are some suggestions that will help you build the courage necessary to flourish in your new undertaking.

Remove from your life any thoughts telling you that you are a victim. When you are creating your own destiny, no one cares if you are a felon. No one cares about your sexual orientation. No one cares about your skin color. No one cares about your past drug or alcohol problems. No one cares how rough you had it as a kid or what type of neighborhood you grew up in. The market for our goods and services doesn't care. All the market cares about is whether we do what we say we can do and whether we provide exceptional service. That's it. I personally won't let my past life become an excuse for not doing my best in this world. I refuse to live in the past. If you didn't like your childhood, don't live there.

Let's look at how smart the drug dealer is. He knows and understands his product; he knows he has a solid customer base. He knows that if he starts selling an inferior product, he will lose his customers. Realize this as well: The dope man is selling poison, yet he succeeds. How is that different from any other business? The answer is "not much." The shame of it is that if the dope man put his efforts into something legal and positive, he would win as well. Are you willing to start exploring your talents and things that might work for you? Take a leap of faith and stay quiet about it. You don't have to share with everyone what you're up to. If what you try doesn't work, no one needs to know the gory details; just try something else.

The "Chicken Soup for the Soul" people were rejected 144 times before someone said yes. Learn to relish rejection; it's the theory of no factor. I promise that if you are willing to do what it takes to win, you will welcome rejection. Never give up; if you get enough "no's," someone will eventually say yes.

Throughout my endeavors, I have been rejected a thousand times. I have complete faith that if I get enough "no's," I will get a yes. I know this for a fact. You're reading this book, aren't you?

Where do the 12 steps of a recovery program fit in here? Let's look back at this reading and see.

Step 1. Admitted we were powerless over our situation and this part of our lives has become unmanageable. When we talked about fear early in this piece, and when I described what kills so many who are addicted, we talked about their fears. While fear may or may not be a life-and-death situation in your case, it is still holding you back. It's the same type of fear that kills the addicted: "the fear of change." Are you willing to admit that you are powerless over your fear of change? Do you dislike your work, friends, and living conditions so much that you know you should change but are afraid to do so because the mere thought terrifies you? I would say, then, that you are powerless over your fear. That fear will prevent you from moving to the next level of your life rendering this part of your life unmanageable.

Step 2. Came to believe that a power greater than yourself could restore you to sanity. Obviously, you are not insane. The point of this step is for you to believe that a power greater than yourself could change your life for the better. For many people, a power greater than themselves is a God of their understanding. For some, a power greater than themselves is a program or a group of people who have learned to over their fear and are now living their life to its fullest potential.

Step 3. Ask you to make a decision to turn your will over to this higher power. If you want to be free of your fears, then you must recognize that what you have been doing has not worked. Do not let your ego hold you back. Make a decision that says to you, I don't see how to change my fear of failure, etc.

Step 4. Ask you to make a fearless and moral inventory of yourself. This means to get honest with yourself. You know inside yourself precisely what you are afraid of. If you think you don't know what the problem is then grab a pen and paper and write down what it could be. You will know in just a couple of minutes what the problem is.

Step 5. Ask you to admit to your higher power and to yourself the exact nature of your wrongs. Do not get caught up in a feeling of guilt. That will hold you back. Think of it in these terms. You admitted you have a problem and your working on fixing it. Do you know how many people will never address their fears? I can answer that from my experience. Most people never reach their maximum potential because they refuse to address their fears. You should feel good about yourself you are taking action.

Step 6. Ask you to become entirely ready to have your higher power rid your life from fear. Whatever your higher power is, be entirely prepared to make the change you need.

Step 7. Ask you to humbly ask your higher power to remove this shortcoming in your life. The key word here is humbly, remember what you have tried before has not worked. The blessing of living a fearless life is based on humility.

Step 8. Ask you to make a list of all persons you have harmed as the result of your fears. If you become emotional thinking about what your fears have cost your family and loved ones, that is normal. It is essential to feel that pain. You don't like pain, and these feelings will help ensure your success in winning your battle over your fears.

Step 9. Ask you to make direct amends to these people whenever possible unless to do so would cause them harm. Please don't overthink this. It may be just a moment between you and your spouse, significant other, etc. Tell the person that you are working on being the best version of you and that you are determined to overcome your fears. It's a huggable moment, and those emotions will make you stronger.

Step 10. Ask you to continue to take a personal inventory and when you are wrong promptly admit it. Please do this to yourself. When you do not follow through or act on an idea recognize it immediately. This builds confidence. Naturally, not all of your ideas or thoughts will turn out to be great things that you need to follow up on. However, stay in a state of awareness and be ready for the great idea that is coming. I want to stress this point. When you continue to be open and fearless in your thinking, there will be an idea that will work.

Step 11. Ask you to seek through prayer and meditation to improve your conscious contact with our higher power. This is a personal thing between you and your higher power. I do want to share that when you do have a great idea and it starts to build into something having quiet time and being grateful will become a must.

Step 12. States that having had a spiritual awakening as a result of these steps that you share what you have learned with others. You have had to reach deep inside yourself to make these changes. Inside of all of us, there is a spirit. Make sure you share a spirit of gratitude by sharing with others your new-found knowledge. If you want to continue to win your battle over your fears giving away what you have learned will ensure that you stay on the right path.

You are now a person of action, and your fears will not dominate you. You have grown past that. You are free of your fears and ready to live a life of freedom. You are free to achieve your destiny.

CHAPTER FOUR

THE DIFFERENCE MAKERS

PART ONE

SHELLY'S GARDEN

The only sound Shelly could hear was her mother's uncontrollable sobbing. The judge had made his decision: guilty of delivering a controlled substance causing death. The next sound Shelly heard was the judge's gavel pounding out the sentence. Shelly would pay the price for her role in the death of a young man.

By all measures, Shelly K had a normal childhood. She was a bright student during her grade school years. In high school, she was an honor roll student and was very involved in school activities. She was also an excellent long-distance runner.

Shelly was popular in school and was always invited to the "everybody's going to be there" type of parties. Alcohol and weed were common at these events, and Shelly was a willing participant. For a lot of these kids, a few beers and a good buzz were plenty, but not for Shelly. She always drank herself into a blackout or a trip to the toilet to throw up her night's fun. There was never a thought that this would turn into anything bigger than that. No one could see that her future would become a bad dream. In fact, it was a nightmare that would leave a man dead.

Out of high school and in the real-world dating scene, Shelly was "out there." Before long, she started dating a local guy who was in a band. Her weekends became a non-stop drug, alcohol, and rock-and-roll party. Cocaine entered the picture during this period of her life. Shelly fell in love twice in short order. First, she fell in love with the man she would eventually marry. Next, she fell in love with the white powder to which she would eventually give her life to and a precursor to a heroin addiction.

The wedding bells chimed in all their glory, and Shelly was now a married woman. Shelly and her husband started their paths together with smiles of joy. The partying on the weekends was as much a part of their lifestyle as was going to work every day. Shelly's husband handled it with ease, but Shelly did not. The weekends turned into weeknights for Shelly. Her fellow workers were partiers, and Shelly fit right in. Time passed without any consequences for her behavior. However, a few fights with the hubby and a few missed work days due to "illness" became routine.

Shelly became pregnant and, upon receiving the news, stopped drinking and drugging immediately. She abstained all nine months of her pregnancy and gave birth to a baby boy. Shelly convinced herself that because she was able to avoid alcohol and drugs, she didn't have a problem. For an addict, that way of thinking usually ends with something bad happening.

For Shelly, the bad came quickly. The day-after-day partying took its toll. She lost her job and, soon after, her marriage. On the loose and heading for disaster, Shelly went wild and ran smack dab into a heroin-filled needle. This was like nothing she had ever felt before. The immediate rush sent waves of "feel good" throughout her body. When the rush was over, it left behind only one thing: the urge for more. So goes the life of the newly addicted. The shadows and dark places become familiar. The hidden faces of the dealers aren't hidden. They offer a smile on the outside, but behind that smile, their real face is exposed. It says, "I got another one."

It started to become clear to Shelly and her ex-husband that she wasn't capable of taking care of herself, let alone their son. With difficulty but in a moment of clarity, Shelly signed over custody of her son. The reality of that action became a weight on Shelly's conscience, and she dragged it around as if it were real. Her only respite from this agony was losing herself in drugs.

Shelly was now part of it all and had become ever-present in the tunnels and dark places that fill the life of a heroin addict. She was willingly accepted among the others; she roamed about their places and dens. She hid from the daylight for fear that the sun's clarity would expose her for the entire world to see. She was malnourished, and her face was sunken. Her once-radiant eyes were glazed over and dull. She dared not look into a mirror for fear that she would slam her face into it and be cut by the shards of her own reflection. Shelly hated herself.

The other addicts' haunts became Shelly's haunts. Time after time, she witnessed mindless parents putting their children in danger. Her mind would scream at her, telling her to run from these people. In these moments of clarity, she imagined it might be a sign from a God...a God she didn't believe in.

Shelly realized she was in trouble. She checked herself into several rehab facilities. She was good for a while and managed to stay clean. It never lasted, she would always use again. Shelly met other addicts and alcoholics and became friends with many of them.

Shelly met a man who was in one of the rehab facilities with her. They stayed in contact and became friends. Her friend was also a heroin addict who only had snorted heroin but had never shot up. Shelly had scored some heroin along with a needle. She explained to her friend how much better mainlining heroin was than snorting it. She helped him shoot up for the first time in his life. The next night, Shelly was back with more heroin. Her friend liked it, so Shelly helped him shoot up again. Not long after his death sentence had been shot into his arm, he fell asleep. Shelly had an intuition that something was wrong, but he was still breathing when she left. For some reason, Shelly felt uneasy. She didn't know why but it all led back to her friend. He never woke up, dying in the same bed.

Shelly was arrested for delivery of a controlled substance causing death. She was out of her mind and detoxed with no help in a jail cell. Shelly was informed that the prosecutor would seek charges for second-degree murder. Shelly was looking at a possible life sentence. She admitted that all she could think about was how she could get dope in prison.

Guilty pleas were agreed to, and the charge ended up being delivery of a controlled substance causing death. Shelly received a 42 month sentence.God appears in our lives in different ways. For Shelly, perhaps it was the instant when everything went white or the sound of the gavel pounding. Perhaps it was carried to her along with the sobs of her mother. It matters not. Before the long ride to prison was over, something had happened. No longer was Shelly's ability to obtain drugs in prison at the forefront of her mind. She recognized that she would have to change her thinking and adapt to a new and cold environment. She was on her own. Once inside, Shelly tried to sign up for any recovery programs available, but none came to pass.

People in recovery need a major distraction to help fill the space in their lives. For Shelly, it came in the form of track shoes and a track on which to run.

Shelly started running on the prison track, which gave her something positive to do. It occupied her time and her mind. For 42 months, she ran until she crossed the finish line. Shelly was committed to changing her life—and change she did.

When Shelly left prison, she found counselors and programs that showed her that addiction recovery wasn't only about not using drugs or alcohol. Rather, it was about developing lifelong coping skills. These are the skills that would teach Shelly a way to live free of the poison that tried to kill her.

Shelly went after sobriety and pursued her formal education with a passion.

She moved forward quickly and was soon working in the recovery field. Shelly had a voice, and she had something to tell the world. Shelly was approached to give a talk at a fundraiser to raise money in support of an addiction recovery project. This was something new to Shelly. In addition to her fear of speaking in front of an audience, she was nervous about telling her story. She had never done that in public, but she hoped that speaking in front of 30 or 40 people would be good for her recovery.

Shelly was given a time and an address. She was stunned when the address took her to the Country Club of Jackson Michigan. How was she going to give her first speech in front of the wealthiest and most influential people in the county? She walked in and was greeted by 150 people instead of the 30 or 40 she had expected.

Shelly had never told her story publicly. She wasn't adept at public speaking. Now she was going to get up on a platform and open her heart and her barely healed wounds to what seemed to be the world. Shelly is a beautiful, thin-framed woman with a smile and a light about her that are hard not to like. I can see her quaking with fear, biting her lip, her mind racing in a thousand directions, dreading the words "Shelly, please come on up."

I am blessed to know Shelly personally. I have watched her tell her story, and I have seen her tears build up until she could hold them back no more. Her complete honesty comes out of every pore of her body. She speaks in a voice whose underlining meaning isn't "look at me and what I did." Instead, the aura that surrounds her says, "Please hear me; my message of hope is for you."

Shelly began telling her story. She was perhaps a little shaky at first, but she settled in. The crowd stared at her in awe. Many members of the audience had no clue this went on in their community. Her voice turned from a little shaky to a steady, heartfelt message that overtook the room. The emotion moved across the place as if it were its own being. It slowly infiltrated everyone's heart, leaving them open and exposed to the hope that Shelly was sharing.

When Shelly was done speaking, even the hardcore and normally stoic businesspeople in attendance couldn't hold back their tears. In fact, they welcomed them as an outlet from the grip that Shelly's story had on them. Shelly's message stunned the crowd. They rose to their feet and the applause was deafening. Shelly was overcome with emotion, not from the crowd, but from the knowledge that the God whom she hadn't believed in for so long had been present in that room. The creator of the universe had opened her heart and she had let him in.

During Shelly's time at the podium, a well-known local artist began to paint, using Shelly's story as a guide and inspiration. The blank and barren canvas gave the artist an opportunity to let her thoughts and feelings flow through her brushes. Little did anyone know what an impact this would have on the audience. Her brushes stroked freely and with ease as if they were gripped by Shelly's truth. The painting would be offered at silent auction. It depicted a garden full of beautiful flowers. At the bottom of the painting was a dark place, symbolizing a life of darkness and despair.

From the bottom to the top, the painting shows how the flowers emerged into the miracle of the sunlight that is recovery. The reference from dark to light is clear and parallels Shelly's life. When Shelly's talk was over, the painting was complete. As if there hadn't been enough tears in that room that night, the artist's brush spoke one more time. It spelled out the title to the piece: "Shelly's Garden."

Shelly doesn't know how much the piece sold for, but the money it raised was significant and unexpected. The hearts of the new owners of "Shelly's Garden" were moved again, as they donated the piece back to its own cause. It still hangs on the walls near Shelly's former office, speaking to all who seek its meaning.

Today, Shelly still tells her story. That story has made Shelley what she is today: a strong, confident woman. And, yes, Shelly still runs. She runs not only because she loves to run but because she knows that this love of running kept her body and mind strong while she was in prison. Shelly still speaks to people in recovery and tells them to "do what you loved to do before you loved drugs." Shelly now competes in long-distance running events and has become a successful competitor.

Shelly remains focused on her recovery, public speaking, and sharing her story, as well as helping others on their journey to recovery.

Shelly and her husband, Mike, are the proud parents of a beautiful little girl. Shelly's son is now back in her life as well.

Shelly has made it to the major leagues of recovery. She didn't make it to the bench because she never even slowed down enough to sit on it. Shelly stepped up to the plate of a life that at one time was thought to be over. She swung hard at her role in helping defeat the curse of addiction. She hit the ball all the way into a blessed and grateful life. Shelly just couldn't stop herself from running around the bases, taking a victory lap that she never stops running. The power of the words of recovery is unparalleled. Use them in your own life and you will receive your own personal power. You will become filled with passion and commitment.

BORDERS

Brad was born and raised in Canada. The problems of addiction and alcoholism are as prevalent there as they are anywhere else in the world. Brad's addiction to drugs led to robbery, drug dealing, and prison.

They parked the get-away car a few blocks away from their intended victim, a sleek blue sedan. They walked quickly and gained a feeling of anticipation with each step, excited to learn what treasures their next conquest might be hiding in its nooks and crannies. While his buddy rifled through the car, Brad stood watch, ready to offer a helping hand if the take was big enough. His friend was almost done, the treasures not yet disclosed, when Brad heard a noise behind him. He spun around to see a figure surging out of the darkness toward them.

The man's face was overtaken by the dark of the night but the baseball bat in his hands was easy to see and its owner's intent was obvious. The scream to run rang true, echoing into the empty streets of 3 a.m. Both took flight at about the same time, an angry pursuer behind them. It seemed like only seconds had passed before the police lights lit up the blackness, their colors darting about in cadence. The lights seemed to circle all around them, trying to encase the now-terrified sprinters.

The chase became a cat-and-mouse game between the now-wanted thieves and law enforcement. They hid and scurried about in the dark streets and shadows. This went on for two hours. This was a time when not everyone had a cell phone; communication wasn't in your hand but came from a stand simply marked "pay phone."

Brad called his girlfriend, who was deeply in love with Brad and willing to do anything to help him escape from his peril. She arrived at the pre-arranged spot and the relieved runners hopped inside her car. Out of breath and scared. They hunkered down as low as the seats would let them. They had only one mission in mind: to get off the streets and go home.

On the way out of the area, they saw police cruisers. With every set of headlights that came toward them, they would duck down and hide their faces. Both breathed a big sigh of relief as they headed down the road. Lying back in their seats, they tried to shake off their fright. Then, out of the dark, the headlights from a vehicle behind them began to approach at a higher-than-normal speed. Before they knew it, the intense white beams of the patrol car's searchlight had hit them. It was as if that white light had carried a message on its beam that simply said, "Caught." Brad would be caught breaking the law many other times, which led to a stay in a state penitentiary.

Brad's story starts in his childhood. He never felt like he fit in anywhere. He hated authority and he was completely out of control. He always refused to behave, leaving his parents baffled.

As far back as Brad can remember, something seemed to be missing in his life. He didn't know what it was exactly, but something was out of sorts and it left him feeling empty. A lot of people think the only way they can fill that void is through drugs and alcohol.

Brad was a hyper-active child. Brad's doctors recommended Ritalin and Adderall, so at an early age he began using drugs to change his behavior. His early teen years were packed with petty crimes. At 16, he was breaking and entering into people's houses and he was headed for trouble.

At 17, Brad was placed by the court into a year-long behavioral rehabilitation center. For the first three months of his stay he was kept fairly isolated. That gave him plenty of time to think about all that he had done. The next nine months were spent outdoors and in a cabin in the woods. Brad enjoyed this step and began taking in all the information he could about how to change. When his year was up, Brad was released and he felt good about himself.

Away at college and on his own, Brad started using alcohol and weed to excess. He recalls that one night, after a party, his friend reached into his pocket and produced a bag filled with white powder. That white powder was cocaine.

Brad's first taste of cocaine ran down his nose and into the back of his throat, infusing his system with its allure and effects. He liked it but didn't immediately go back for more. The following weekend, he hooked up with his friend and they went to find the dope man...and more cocaine. At age 19, Brad started his journey into addiction, drug-related crime, and a life of misery.

Brad's newly acquired taste for cocaine escalated from a weekend thing to a daily activity. Brad was high in class all the time and his grades began to decline at a rate that could be choreographed. Brad's behavior caused the alarm bells to go off for his professors and the dean. It didn't take long before Brad was expelled from school due to his unacceptable grade point average.

Brad's new sense of freedom was accompanied by a sense of failure at school. He landed a commission-based job and excelled at it. Brad had become a car salesman and doing cocaine before and during work was his ritual. Cocaine gave Brad an added buzz when he sold a car. His brain was already humming in response to the cocaine; he felt invincible and powerful. Most of the public didn't recognize this. They thought he was just a pumped-up salesman and full of energy. They were right, but his energy came from a dope dealer.

Self-sabotage is custom-made for the addicted. Brad was making $60,000 a year selling cars and had plenty of money to buy all the dope he wanted. Slowly but surely, he began to sabotage this blessing. Brad stopped going to work and he eventually lost his job.

Brad was thrown out of his apartment and took refuge on his brother's couch. He worked at a couple of small jobs but got run off by the ownership for all the same reasons. Brad was high all the time.

Pills of all colors and flavors consumer Brad's life. Some days he would take 30 or 40. Brad's brother wasn't happy about any of Brad's actions and there were times when Brad's brother had had enough. Brad was close to losing his two-by-six rented couch space due to lack of respect and payment. The order from Brad's brother was clear: Clean up or get out.

Brad knew he was in trouble, so he reached out to his grandparents as a last gasp of hope. His grandparents flew him to Florida to attend a thousand-dollar-a-day rehab facility. When he got out of rehab, Brad flew back to Canada, where he started using drugs right away. His drug dealer friend had grown tired of selling cocaine and had achieved a new status among his peers by upgrading to his drug of choice: heroin.

The seduction of heroin came easy for Brad. Its allure comes across quite easily with the opportunity to simply snort it instead of shoot it. Brad has been snorting cocaine for years, so rolling a dollar bill into a tube through which to snort drugs came naturally to him. Brad snorted heroin for a while but that didn't last long. Soon he was sticking a needle into his arm and shooting up heroin.

Brad's family could not tolerate his actions. He was asked to leave his brother's house and he became homeless. The streets became Brad's way of life. He did drugs, sold drugs, and lived as a drug addict.

Finally, Brad grew tired of being sick and tired. Some of Brad's family lived in North Carolina. Brad has visited them there and loved it. When an opportunity arose to fly to North Carolina to join his family and friends, Brad jumped at it. He had been trying to stay clean and experienced some limited success. Brad had been on a crime spree to help feed his expensive habit. During that time, he had acquired two felony convictions. Little did Brad know he was about to face another one.

January 11, 2010 started with an air of excitement for Brad. He was going to board a plane in Canada and return to his beloved North Carolina. He had always felt like it was home, and he missed it.

As Brad's trip to the airport began, he developed an odd set of feelings. He felt guilty, but about what? Brad's feelings of guilt migrated from his thoughts and started established a stronghold deep in his gut. His stomach churned and he would become almost paralyzed by the end of his trip.

At the Canadian airport, Brad's trip through US Customs did not go as smoothly as usual. The customs agents seemed to ask more questions than normal. It seemed to him that they looked at him differently and with a suspicious eye. Brad had been through customs many times, and this felt very different. The question that ran through his mind while in flight was "Am I just being paranoid?"

The tension in Brad's body began to increase as the plane started its final descent. On the tarmac, Brad's mind ran at an uncontrollable speed. Thoughts came and went, his palms sweated, and his heart raced.

When Brad exited the plane and entered the airport, he felt relieved that there was no sign of danger. When he walked into the luggage area, the chills that had temporarily left his body returned.

The worry that had "owned him" was back, overwhelming his senses with a feeling that he described as terrifying. Standing there with Brad's picture in their hands were three police officers. Eye contact as made, and that was that.

Brad was arrested for six counts of drug trafficking. When most people hear the words "drug trafficking," they think about large amounts of drugs. That wasn't the case here, Brad had sold small amounts of drugs to an undercover police officer. A little here and little there was his downfall. They had met on numerous occasions, which showed a consistent pattern of possession with intent to distribute.

Brad was sentenced to one year in a North Carolina penitentiary. Because he was a Canadian citizen, part of his sentence was deportation to Canada. After Brad had completed his one-year prison sentence, he was banned from the United States forever.

Brad was now committed to changing his life. While incarcerated, he had read everything available to him on the subject of addiction recovery. He had two goals when he got out and the prison doors closed behind him. One was to get a German Shepherd, and the other was to become an addiction counselor.

Brad went to work on himself and his goals. He educated himself and spent five years as a full-time addiction counselor. He obtained a beautiful German Shepherd dog along the way.

His next move was big and scary. Brad decided to make his way in the recovery field using social media, which offered him access to a large and willing audience.

Brad became an enormous presence on Facebook and Instagram. He offers live recovery counseling on a one-on-one basis. Brad has hosted multiple interviews with experts in the field of addiction recovery. On his social media outlets, he posts powerful and positive videos almost daily. Brad has reached thousands and is making a difference.

Yes, Brad McLeod has found the light. He is married and has a son whom he treasures. I am honored to know him and honored that the granted me this interview.

Brad got off the bench of the average. He stood up to the plate of a future filled with massive personal growth and sobriety. He has hit a home run across Canada over into a country that shunned him.

Do you see any parallels in Brad's story that you can relate to in your own life? If you are reading this book, you are a person who is interested in personal growth.

Brad has taken his social media presence to a new level. The literal operations of these platforms are difficult to understand. Paths and sequences must be learned and followed, and all are mandatory to create this kind of presence.

Brad has put in the effort; he has spent hours learning and understanding what makes these outlets work. It has been a trial-and-error process that at times was well beyond frustrating. Brad has dedicated his life to higher learning and is living his dream of being his own boss.

The wisdom here is this. Brad started on the bottom. He knew very little about the internet. Brad's drive comes from his passion for helping others. Everyone who wakes up thinking about their dream and who then takes consistent action toward it will win.

Brad's recovery is full of step work that he has used from different 12-step recovery programs. Brad uses their words of success in addiction recovery to fit his situation. An example of this fact is that Brad came to believe that a power greater than himself could guide him through his challenges in obtaining social media knowledge and getting his message across to thousands. That knowledge keeps him grounded and humble. He has used the twelfth step of many 12-step programs; he understands that now that he has assumed his current position in life, he must share his knowledge with others to continue being a blessing to the world. Brad gives away his knowledge so that he can grow.

Brad McLeod's social media outlets are vast as well as his services. Brad can be easily found by doing a search on Facebook or Instagram. You will see how he has had a real impact in the field of addiction recovery.

BROTHER MARK

Smoking crack to get up and doing heroin to come down, Mark led a wild lifestyle that didn't appear to have an end.

Mark's childhood home was average. His father, a hardworking old-school type of gentleman, was quiet, and showed little affection to his children. Mark's need for attention came naturally; he was starved for it.

Like a lot of other kids with the same problem, Mark began acting out. Mark will be the first to admit that his decisions were all his. He now takes full responsibility for his actions and their consequences. He doesn't blame anyone but himself for the shape his life took.

The first feeling of relief came when Mark was 12. He began hanging around older kids, trying to gain approval and acceptance. He began using both drugs and alcohol. As it is with so many, that sense of belonging was like taking a breath of new life. At last, Mark felt like he fit in.

When Mark got out of school and on his own, his use of drugs, alcohol, and sex escalated. It was twisting and turning in his mind like a circle that never stops. He always craved more. His lust to change how he felt both physically and mentally guided his life like a compass pointing toward disaster.

Mark had several failed marriages. His vows were always broken, and he led a life of the selfish and of the lost. Naturally, he bounced from job to job, and he sabotaged everything good in his life.

Finally landing his dream job, Mark worked his way up to manager at a very successful strip club. This became part of his already torn and shattered life for 20 years. It was 20 years of ups and downs, 20 long years of orchestrating a world of the desperate. Many of the women in the club were addicted to drugs and alcohol and they felt like they had no choice. Their despair and shame were felt at the end of every shift.

Many nights Mark would stare into the audience, feeling disgusted by the clientele? Brief moments of regret would flash through his mind, as he knew that his job's main role was to be uncaring. He looked into the wild eyes of his patrons, who could look but never touch. They always left in time to clean themselves up before returning home to their wives and children.

The change in Mark's life started when he attended a bachelor party – oddly enough, at another strip club. The details are sketchy but this is what we do know: Mark ended up in the back room with a prostitute whom he refused to pay. That was the beginning of the end. Mark was arrested for rape along with other sex-related charges.

Mark sat at his rape trial with years of bad decisions running down his face, staining his cheeks bright red. The jury was out, and his destiny was in their hands.

After a long and painful wait, the jury came back to read his future. "Hung jury" was the verdict. The judge declared a mistrial on the rape charge. However, there were other charges to be dealt with and Mark prepared for the worst. He pleaded out on the offense of having sex in a public place. Mark was stunned by the fact that he would now be put on the registered sex offender list for 10 years. He had reached a bottom so deep, his mind constantly recreated all the hurt and pain he had caused.

Little did Mark know that soon an event would change his life forever. It was full of forgiveness, love, and the grace of the God of the universe, a God who was not done with Mark.

One day, Mark was flipping through the channels when he ended up tuned into a local TV ministry. He recalls this as if it were yesterday. The remote quit working and he just sat and watched. His spirit longed for something to cling to, something real and something good.

He told his girlfriend (now his wife) that he was going down to that church to check these people out. He was grasping at any opportunity to ease his guilt-filled mind, anything that could create some hope in his life.

Having grown up in a Catholic home, Mark admits that he had some knowledge of God but had never put it into practice. He felt there was a God, but not for men as guilty as he was. When Mark walked into that church, he found a true sanctuary of peace. He felt love and warmth envelop him like a mist of pure serenity and hope.

Talking with some members of the church, Mark felt something that he had not felt in a very long time: the amazing feeling of unconditional love and a spirit full of new beginnings. Mark turned his life over to the God of his understanding, and the transformation began. At last, he had gotten what he had always wanted: He was accepted.

Mark's spirit of giving to others may have appeared small to someone from the outside looking in. He would pick up people who needed a ride to church. He would show love to homeless people by offering them a free "all-you-can-eat" meal if they came to church with him. He began participating in church activities and gaining the trust of his new friends. He wanted the peace and joy that the others had, and God's message to him was to do for others.

Mark started with a vision of being able to get a little place that he could operate and use to spread God's love and the freedom from addiction. Let us all remember the Mark of a few paragraphs ago: hopeless, full of fear, tortured by his inability to forgive himself, and desperate to feel better.

Mark had no money. His credit was terrible and he had recently been forced into bankruptcy. His ability to create something more in his life seemed nonexistent. The only thing he had was his newly found faith.

One day, Mark was driving around and dreaming. He passed a small commercial plaza and noticed a moving van in front of one of the small units. Something told him to stop and talk to the people who were moving out.

He approached the strangers with guarded enthusiasm. They were very friendly as Mark explained that he was looking for a small and cheap space to rent. All the while, he kept in mind that he didn't have enough money for even the smallest of spaces. The kind folks said, "Let's call the owner and see if he can help you." With nothing to lose, Mark agreed.

He was stunned by the outcome of that shot-in-the-dark phone call. The owner was a member of Mark's new church. The owner told the tenant, "Give him the keys; and we'll work out the details later." You can imagine the joy in Marks' heart as God began opening new doors in his life – a life committed to giving back to God's world.

Sixteen years later, Mark's little space has grown so that he now owns the entire building. He helps people in the immediate area by providing necessities and a place to get out of the weather. A section gives away clothes, and a meeting room offers hope of God's love and forgiveness to the addict, the alcoholic, and so many more.

Mark receives no government funding of any kind. The building is completely supported by a couple of philanthropists who are now Mark's friends. Mark has always been a big thinker; he has tried several fundraising ideas, to no avail. His explanation is simple: "We could always use more, but by grace, we have all we need."

"It's God's plan, not mine."

Mark crawled to the bench of the big leagues one day at a time. As he got stronger, he walked up to the plate and hit a line drive at local pain and suffering. He hit it in the right direction, into God's hands.

MEDICINE MAN

"You can have all the drugs and alcohol you want. You can talk to the greatest therapist in the world. You can have all the money you want and all the trappings that it provides, but none of this will make you like you," stated S at the beginning of our interview.

On Tuesday September 11, 2001, America was shaken by the images that were replayed again and again. The tragedy sounded its own alarm with a dust-filled sky. The cries of loss and anger rang forth, if not out loud, then from Americans' broken hearts. The shadows of the World Trade Center were there and then they were not. There were many lives there, and then they were not. America's soul felt a new burning hole with each replay. She had been sucker-punched. We could do nothing but watch as the planes led by hatred crashed into the Twin Towers, leaving a scar that even today refuses to heal.

That day, the plea for help at Ground Zero rang loud and true. S, along with other paramedics and rescue personnel, was on his way to the crime scene. They left Jersey City via boat, destined for Manhattan. En route, it seemed that everyone was getting drunk. S thought to himself, 'We're on our way to help people, and they're all wasted.' He then realized, at that moment, he wasn't alone. There were others who didn't like themselves and who had resorted to drugs and alcohol to change the way they felt. S himself had arrived at many life-and-death emergencies under the influence of drugs.

S starts his story, "I was the youngest of three twins, and I guess I always thought of myself as the crap leftover. I didn't like myself, and I didn't like the things I was supposed to like. I didn't feel like I belonged. I felt isolated and different." S was an awkward kid who was bullied on a regular basis. As S shared these events with me, I could hear a twinge in his voice as he bared his truth.

S had trouble trusting people. He had been picked on for so long that he naturally repelled anyone who approached him as a potential friend. He wanted to fit in, but S could never picture himself fitting in anywhere.

When S was 14, his guidance counselor introduced him to a new kid at school who was involved with a youth ministry group. His new friend introduced S to the other kids and the leaders of the organization. One of the leaders was charismatic and seemed cool to a kid who was shy and untrusting. The leader took an interest in S and seemed to be very accepting. This felt new to S. He thought, 'Finally, I'm in a place that accepts me.' One day, all the kids were hanging around the leader's house. Everything was going smoothly, and S was having a good time.

The leader of the group who had taken an interest in S had an ulterior motive. When they were off to the side of the group, the leader tried to make a sexual move on S. S told him no and left.

The organization in which the team leader was involved was a national one and very recognizable. S refused to feel like a helpless victim. He reported this man's attempt to molest him and expected that legal action would be taken against him. When S revealed the truth, he was called a liar. The organization went into full denial mode and refused to take any action.

This rattled S, who had dealt with trust issues all his life. He felt abandoned by his friends and everyone involved with that organization. These feelings would fuel the flame of things to come.

This was a dark time in S's life. Inner turmoil filled his mind. Negative thoughts rotated in his brain like a twister, nonstop and relentless. S wanted desperately to change how he felt about himself, so he began experimenting with drugs.

Life went on and S began a career as a paramedic, holding certifications in both New Jersey and Pennsylvania. He smoked marijuana every day as well as any other drugs he could get his hands on. At the same time, S was responding to life-and-death calls.

S's hopes surged, and he was full of anticipation whenever the station house received an emergency call involving a senior citizen. Excited, he never knew what surprises awaited him in the next medicine cabinet. He wished the ambulance's swirling lights would swirl bigger, he wished the sirens would scream louder, and most of all he wished they would get there faster.

While his partner attended to the victim, S would ask to see the person's medications. Of course, they were always in the bathroom medicine cabinet. There, his excitement was rewarded.

Prescription narcotics were his prize. Nearly all seniors had pain medications. S took his time and was thorough. He stole the prescription pain pills without remorse, knowing that the person being rushed to the hospital would receive more.

S's addiction to prescription drugs created havoc in his life. With his inability to count on rescue calls for his dope and to afford the cost of buying them on the street, S remarked, "I started shooting heroin for economic reasons."

One night while S was still working as a paramedic in New Jersey, he stopped along a side street to shoot up heroin. The frigid air of four o'clock in the morning was the first thing S felt when the Narcan awoke his dying body. He was found near death in his car with no recollection of how he had gotten there. With his mind beginning to clear, he recognized the paramedic who had saved him. It was someone with whom S used to work, and the embarrassment was soon replaced by gratitude. S lost his job and his New Jersey certification, but he was still certified in Pennsylvania.

S picked himself up and went to Pennsylvania. He was offered a job almost immediately. When he was asked why he had left his last job, S lied and said nothing about the actual reason. He was hired and looked forward to a new start. The new start didn't last very long. S was high on heroin, and he drove dangerously on the way to a rescue. When he returned to the station, his partner reported him immediately. S was fired and barely escaped prosecution.

S decided to try and get well. He spent a year in a Florida rehab house. He did well until the sudden urge to return home hit him. Within two days, S had relapsed and OD'd in his parents' living room.

Something had to give. Time after time, S had counted on his parents to bail him out. The mental strain exhausted his parents. As a means of survival, his parents were attending groups like Co-

Dependents Anonymous. They were done helping S dig his own grave.

S made a decision; he was going to do something different with his life. He located a responsible doctor and began a Suboxone maintenance program. The drug Suboxone is used to help ease the withdrawal symptoms of heroin. It was time to make a change, and S took charge of his life.

Recovery Centers, 30-day, 60-day, and 90-day programs came and went. Twelve-step meetings of all kinds were on the menu, and S dug into the mix.

At these meetings, people would announce themselves as alcoholics and drug addicts. S knew that he could no longer be labeled a drug addict or alcoholic. He felt that the repetitive nature of people announcing themselves as their disease wouldn't work for him. He had to be himself. He wasn't his disease; he was a human being with an addiction problem. S states with sincerity and no judgment, "If this is working for you, please continue; we are all different." S's work paid off and he is now a person in long-term recovery.

S says that acceptance is the key to his serenity. He likes himself these days and is free to be who he is. When he accepted this, his life got better. S became a true father and now spends as much time as possible with his children. S is engaged to a woman who stuck by him through thick and thin.

S states that his fiancée's family wanted nothing to do with him at first. He earned their trust through his actions and is now welcome in their lives. He felt loved and was able to realize that all the horrible things in his past made him the man he is today and established the purpose that God had for him all along. S gives all the credit to the God of his understanding and he has lived the 12 steps of recovery for years.

In 2006, S saw the noted public speaker and author Les Brown speak. At that moment, God's presence and S's mind came together. God had put a dream on the inside of S, and he knew in his heart that he was born to be a speaker.

Free to pursue his dreams, S began taking action. First, he realized that there had to be other first responders like him. He began looking for a podcast dedicated to supporting first responders with substance abuse issues. He was shocked to find none.

S is a man of action. He developed a podcast called Rescue the Rescuer. S is now Director of Network Development for Mental Health News Radio Network and President of Rescued Consulting. S is a public speaker and travels the country, speaking to various groups and sharing the good news of recovery. He reinforces the "If I can do it, so can you" ideology. S creates videos addressing addiction issues. At the time of this writing, S had just done a video for The National Centers for Addiction.

S created a consulting firm, through which he works with various treatment firms on marketing, etc. He will work only with treatment centers he believes in. S lives by a code: If you help enough people get what they want, you will get what you want.

Stephen Kavalkovich is one of the superstars of addiction recovery and mental health.

Stephen has made it to the major leagues. He got off the bench and stepped up to the plate of God's plan. He hit a grand slam over the wall of what seemed impossible.

Contact Info for Stephen Kavalkovich

Facebook pages: Stephen Kavalkovich Rescue the Rescuer Program/Rescued Consulting

LinkedIn: Stephen Kavalkovich

Instagram: steve_kavalkovich Rescued Consulting LLC

Twitter: Stephenrescues Rescued Consulting

Websites:

www.rescuetherescuer.com

www.Mhnrnetwork.com

Email: Stephen@rescuetherescuer.com

For more information, contact:
www.mentalhealthnewsradionetwork.com

Speaking engagement information: 1-856-924-9360

THE WINDY CITY

Some children get lost in the foster care system. JW was one of them. He was a ward of the state from ages two to eleven. His mother had to give him up, as she was institutionalized for a serious mental issue. His father was married to another woman and was long gone.

JW felt abandoned. He started out living with a few different relatives. His relatives gave up on him and he was placed in one foster home after another. He created havoc and chaos everywhere he went. He was kicked out of every grade school he attended. He would not make it into high school.

At age 12, JW ended up moving in with his "ganged-up" cousin on the West Side of Chicago. He jumped right into the gang lifestyle. Over the next four years, he was shot three times and stabbed four times.

By the age of 14, JW not only was a gang member but had quickly moved up in rank. The West Side of Chicago is overrun with gangs and gang violence; life on the street is dangerous. His fellow gang members scorned JW because he had risen so fast. On "his" corner, he sold dope to kids from the suburbs, who came to him because he was white; his race built a false sense of trust among them. He was one of the few white people in his predominantly black gang. This built another layer of distrust among his fellow gang members. It became such a problem that he needed a crew of fellow gang members with him as he worked his corner. Everyone in the crew was what he called "strapped down." Simply stated, everyone in his crew had a gun, including himself.

JW became addicted to cocaine during this time in his life. His success as a drug dealer made it easy for him to buy as much cocaine as he wanted. JW didn't fall into the trap of becoming his best customer. He kept a close eye on his own addiction and was able to make clear and concise decisions when it came to his own drug-dealing business.

The stress of being on constant alert every moment of every day was real. The entire commerce of this area thrived on three things: illegal guns, drug money, and drugs. No one, including JW's peers, could be trusted. He had to watch his back, even if one of his fellow gang members was behind him. Potential danger was everywhere around him; it came from so many angles that taking any moment to relax could end up with an arrest or death.

Daily shootings on the West Side of Chicago were as common as the weather report. It was an occupational hazard for all who chose JW's profession. Illegal guns were everywhere, and as easily obtained as a pack of gum.

Getting out of your comfort zone, in this case, meant leaving your area to buy drugs. A shortage of drugs caused JW to risk the consequences of leaving his zone. A contact in another area was found and a meeting was arranged at their apartment complex.

Once JW arrived at the contact's apartment, he was told they would have to go behind the complex to complete the transaction. The given reason was that the police were watching his every move.

Immediately, JW's personal red flags sprang up. He had a bad feeling deep inside his gut; he didn't feel right about any of this.

He was carrying $400 in cash to complete the transaction. Unfortunately, JW didn't listen to any of the red flags. He and the dealer ended up behind a fence, relatively secluded.

The two of them faced each other to start the dope deal. The seller had a vivid plan in his mind that was going to leave him with his dope and $400 of JW's money. He quivered about, his eyes like those of a predator, taking in all that was around him. JW, too, was uncomfortable. Though he hadn't yet connected all the dots, he had left himself vulnerable.

The man pulled a gun on JW. JW's primal instincts from his street life came without thought. He grabbed the gun and tried to twist it out of the thief's hand. A gun blast rang loud throughout the neighborhood, the bullet hit JW in the leg. JW's efforts to take away the gun were rewarded; he managed to get the gun away from his would-be killer. Within a second, JW was able to pull out his own gun. He pointed the gun directly at the assailant and the attacker recognized his impending doom. With a look of disgust in his eyes, the murderous drug dealer turned and walked away.

JW knew he had a prize even though he was still lying on the ground. A fully automatic Mac 10 was the prize and a clip that held 60 rounds was a bonus. JW had all 60 rounds, though unfortunately one of them was an unwelcome intruder in his leg.

Now the madness of JW's cocaine addiction kicked into full gear and owned his thought process. His mind was spinning as he tried to decide what to do next. While still on the ground, he called a friend to come get him. Soon help arrived. When clear of the danger zone, the conniving mind of the addicted went to work and they struck up a deal. The devil is in the doing; JW traded the gun for an undisclosed amount of cocaine. JW spent the next two days stoned out of his mind and numb. This was the only way he could keep down the nagging throb that shot through his leg with every heartbeat. He constantly embraced the white powder to dilute the unbearable pain.

Finally, JW could take no more. He went to the emergency room of a nearby hospital. The sterile feel of the bright lights in the hospital room seemed more intrusive than welcoming. He relented to its coldness and accepted the help he needed. When the nurse took his blood pressure and pulse, she remarked, "You must really be in pain because your heart is racing out of control and your blood pressure is off the charts." He wasn't about to tell her that his body was reeling out of control because his system was overrun with cocaine. The bullet was removed, and his leg patched up. The doctor administered a shot of Dilaudid, having no idea that JW had a significant amount of coke in his system. Adding the drug Dilaudid to cocaine is called "speedballing" because of its immediate effect on the addict's system. In just a minute or two, JW threw up all over the room and then left the hospital. JW now recognized the absolute insanity of all this and saw how unmanageable his life had become.

Most violence and incidents involving guns are attempts by one dope dealer to rob another or attempts by civilians to steal dope. In all, JW was threatened with a gun 12 times. Nine of those times, he took the gun from the perpetrator. The other three times, he was shot but never in vital organs.

Being shot is one thing but JW's woes didn't stop there. He was stabbed on four different occasions. JW really liked to skateboard and it was an activity that fit in well with his "job." He could dodge in and out of places and escape danger if necessary. One of JW's rules was to never go out on the street without his gun. One time, he broke this rule and it nearly cost him his life.

One clear and warm afternoon, JW was riding his skateboard when, out of nowhere, four guys jumped out from behind a car and "clotheslined him." His skateboard flew out from under him and hit the car tire, then ricocheted back and hit him. One guy pulled out a gun, another a knife, while the others pulled JW's hoodie over his face. Their mission was clear, as they began punching and kicking him. They were out to mess up somebody and to rob them. For JW, this was another occupational hazard.

JW is a survivor. His instincts went into life-or-death survival mode as he began to fight his way out of this brutal attack.

Grabbing his skateboard, he swung at the gun and knocked it out of his attacker's hand. In an instant, he was on his feet and came up swinging. The man with the gun and the other two men took off running, leaving behind one enraged attacker with the knife. JW was now more angry than afraid.

JW took big swings with his board, missing the assailant twice. On his next swing, he felt the steel of the knife sink between his ribs. JW never relented. He managed to hit the guy's leg hard with his board. After that, the blade man took off. The miracle of the stab wound was that it didn't hit any of JW's vitals and required only six stitches to close.

Over the next few years, JW was in trouble with the law and his list of felonies grew. His multiple felonies resulted in multiple prison stints. Though he was incarcerated, JW always ganged up with members of his outside gang who were on the inside.

His last prison stay broke him. JW spent ten and a half months in lockdown. He spent 21 hours a day in a small cell created to give someone time to think. For JW, it was a nightmare. He made up his mind that this was it. When he was released, he had nothing but the clothes on his back and a commitment to never return.

JW began attending multiple recovery meetings and found a sponsor to help him with his drug addictions, which were many. He was living in a halfway house that gave him a greatly appreciated roof over his head.

JW had very few job skills, but he remembered helping someone repair their plumbing and he had enjoyed it. Opening a Chicago phone book, he began calling one plumber after another to see if they needed any help. The typical answer was no; however, he kept trying until, finally, someone said yes.

Before he hung up the phone, JW came clean with the owner about his past. The owner must have been moved or guided because he asked JW to report to work the next day and to have his work boots on.

Work boots! JW didn't have any work boots! The shelter where he was staying had an area where people could drop off clothes, shoes, and other items to help those in need. JW needed work boots badly. He went down to the drop-off area and, to his amazement, discovered that someone had dropped off boots that fit him perfectly. I don't know if you believe in divine intervention but...

Today JW is still with that company. He is entrusted with everything and he has full access to anything he needs: vans, parts, the office, etc. He is a journeyman plumber and works nonstop but that's not the end of his story.

JW is changing and saving lives all over Chicago. His energy and passion for the recovery movement is amazing.

He is involved in the North City area Narcotics Anonymous, which allows him to speak at treatment centers and detox centers all over the Chicagoland area. He has been asked to speak at various law enforcement events. JW goes to schools to tell his story. He is involved in several outreach and non-profit programs that help find addicts without insurance who want to go to treatment centers. He does a live Facebook recovery program every Monday night at 8:00 p.m. CST. He is the administrator of five Facebook pages and heads up his own page, called Chicago Hope Dealers. He is a mentor, a teacher, and someone who wants to give back what was freely given to him. JW lives the 12 steps of Alcoholics Anonymous, not only in his addiction recovery but in his everyday life. He is happy.

JW got off the bench of gang life, stepped up to the plate of hope, and hit the ball across one of the greatest cities in the country. Yes, Jonathon Weirich is living a life of recovery that he would never have dreamed was possible. You can contact him through any of his social media sites.

Most grocery stores have a section that is labeled "damaged goods." These products are mostly cans, that have been dented and scratched, so they are discounted. When we look at these cans, we judge them based on their outsides. Here's the good news: Like JW, they are just as good on the inside as the cans that are perfect. What's inside of you matters. Don't let yourself believe that you are "damaged goods." We have all been dinged up and scratched by life. Take off the label of "damaged goods" and walk into the light of the forgiven and blessed. When you do this, you can live your life to your fullest potential and create your own destiny. Live with passion! Work the steps of any 12- step program. Change the words to fit your situation and step into your freedom.

CHAPTER FIVE

FOR THE LOVE OF FOOD

INTO THE FRYING PAN

When Jesse got locked up, he detoxed on the cold, dirty floor that had served as the starting point for many before him. It was the floor of deep despair and pain that most can't imagine. The reality is, the bottom of addiction has a floor. For some, the bottom is prison; they are left and lost in the cold bureaucracy of a system that doesn't even know they are there. For others, the cemetery is their refuge from the struggle and pain. Their dreams and potential are buried; sealed in forever is a life that should have and could have been.

Born in South Florida, Jesse was surrounded by the sights, sounds, and flavors for which this region of Florida is known. He immersed himself in a desire to learn everything he could about cooking and food. He received a culinary degree from Atlantic Technical Center and went on to work in some of Florida's top kitchens.

In a world full of people who can't seem to find their path, it's such a joy when someone like young Jesse never wavered from his passion for food. Some of Jesse's fondest memories are of him watching his beloved grandmother in the kitchen. The simplest things she did – such as peeling an apple with a paring knife – captivated him.

There was a feeling of calm in the kitchen. It seemed to overtake the rowdy and sometimes wild youngster. Jesse felt at peace surrounded by the sights and the warm smells in his favorite room of the house.

Trying to relive those wonderful, calming memories, he pursued his passion for food and cooking. It was always about the food, always about the technique, always about the ingredients and always a desire to excel at his God-given gift.

Jesse never wanted to play with the same things other kids did; he wasn't interested. However, he did want to be part of something, and he wanted to fit in with others his age. He recalls smoking pot at the age of 12. He liked it. He had found his way out of the feeling that he was different from everybody else. He recalls his first time getting high: "As if the clouds had parted was the feeling." It was the feeling Jesse would desperately chase for years to come. It was the feeling that many others chase, only to discover the cost of catching it.

At age 16, Jesse was going at it hard, both in the kitchen and in his climb from one drug to another. He was "a-rockin' and a-rollin'" right along with the other members of the kitchen staff.

The food service and the professional chef industry is certainly not exempt from drug addiction and alcohol problems. In fact, it has among the highest rates of alcoholism and drug addiction. Tony Bourdain described this in his New York Times bestselling book "Kitchen Confidential." It is very common for all the staff from different restaurants and eateries to meet up at nightclubs after they have ended their shifts and closed for the night.

For many of these culinary warriors, partying into the night and then sleeping for the better part of the next day becomes a cycle. They wake up, shake it off, and get ready to do it again. It may seem harmless at first but before they know it, a lifestyle of addiction develops.

Jesse began his journey after graduating from culinary school. He worked his way up in some very nice restaurants throughout Florida. Doing what had to be done is a young chef's duty. Jesse knew this, so he started his true professional career in the trenches with all the other rookies. Jesse had talent, so before his run was over, he was working in some of the top high-end restaurants in Florida. He had made a name for himself. Gifted and passionate to a fault, some chefs like Jesse are so driven, they become almost monsters. They are wrapped in a vision of what the food should be and are puzzled that everyone else can't see it that way. They are sometimes haunted by the false vision that their food validates who they are. They seem to see food in a different light, as if each dish is making its own significant statement for all the world to see and hear. Jesse sought relief from his passion in either a bottle or a substance.

Jesse went from smoking marijuana daily to prescription opiates. Pills of any flavor, acid, mushrooms, Xanax, and Valium came easily. He recalls drinking over-the-counter alcohol-laced cough syrup during the middle of the day. He tried anything and everything; the pot just wouldn't get him high anymore. Jesse turned into a thief. If he visited someone's house, the first thing he did was go to the bathroom. There, he methodically took inventory of the medicine cabinet, stealing anything he thought would get him high.

A lot of things were happening in Jesse's life. He was still working and cooking. Like many alcoholics and addicts, he felt he was functional and normal. Jesse began jumping from job to job. His irresponsible and irrational behavior proved that he wasn't functional or normal. After a few years, this behavior caught up with Jesse. That's when his life began to crumble.

Jesse could no longer conduct himself in a civil or responsible manner. His life was on the ropes. The drink and the drugs had taken Jesse away from all that he had once held dear. The truth is the truth; addiction doesn't take away anything the addict doesn't willingly give it. The progression of addiction can seemingly be charted. It's like looking at an evolutionary chart in reverse.

Near the end, Jesse was shooting heroin, smoking crack, and living like a zombie, dead but alive. He had been arrested several times but always for something minor. He was sleeping outside and panhandling for his dope money. Everything he had achieved in the industry he loved was gone. Gone were his work, his family, his passion for anything except getting high. Staring into the eyes of the person he used to be, he still caught glimpses of his former self, but when he reached out to touch his old life, it disappeared into the black. Jesse had been in and out of rehab numerous times but nothing stuck.

On a warm and damp day, Jesse sat dope sick on the curb. He was scared, scrawny, and lost. He watched as who he now can see was a messenger from God roll up in a squad car. Jesse was too sick to run. When the arresting officer got him in the car, Jesse was smiling. When asked why, Jesse said, "I'm going to jail and I'm going to get my life back."

Jesse had found his bottom. He admitted that he was powerless over his addictions and that his life had become unmanageable. A brief instant of clarity came back to Jesse's mind. He asked to be transferred to a 90-day rehab program within the jail.

Jesse recalls sitting in a 12-step meeting the first night he arrived. In his past life Jesse had attended many recovery meetings but he had done all of them to please either the court system or his family and friends. He had never attended a meeting for himself. This one was different. He sat listening to another addict share his story. Jesse thought to himself, 'Hey, he's telling my story, my exact story.' It sent chills through him as the reality of what he had done looked right back at him.

Jesse was ready this time. With his soul wide open and vulnerable, he let recovery take over his life. He describes having a spiritual awakening of sorts. He doesn't care what anyone calls it; he knows something just happened.

Jesse became a new man; he was on fire and thirsty for more. Out of jail at last, Jesse took the actions of a person who wants to get well. He moved into a 12-step house, got a sponsor, and attended two meetings a day.

Jesse got involved in everything related to recovery. He got a work release and started doing what he had been put on this world to do. He was cooking and growing stronger in his mind. His true passion started to rebuild his core. He was able to direct his energy and his natural drive toward something good again.

Jesse Schenker is a superstar of recovery. He is also a superstar businessman and chef. In 10 short years of sobriety, Jesse Schenker changed his life forever, one day at a time. He is now married with two children. When Jesse got clean, he was broke, both spiritually and financially. He worked, prayed, and never relented in achieving his dream. He formerly owned two restaurants in New York and now owns a restaurant/catering service named 2 Spring, a modern American brasserie, located in Oyster Bay, NY. He declares what his life is today: "It's unimaginable, it's beyond my wildest dreams." The amount of gratitude that surges out of someone who is truly grateful is gratifying to be around. Jesse still tries to attend as many meetings as his hectic life will allow.

This man got off the bench, stepped back up to the plate of making his dreams come true. He swung at creating a life free from drugs and alcohol. Jesse swung so hard, he hit it clear over New York City and landed it in Oyster Bay. Jesse and his family are living the promises of recovery.

Jesse had a spiritual awakening as the result of following and working his 12-step program. Becoming humble enough to admit you need help is a wonderful beginning of your journey. If you have tried everything you can think of and you are still not getting the results you want, what are you willing to do to get there? Jesse finally gave in and now he is winning.

A TRIP AROUND THE WORLD

Andy lived like an animal. He took up residence in an abandoned building. Its outer appearance, once filled with dreams, sagged under the weight of the hopeless. He was filthy, both in his person and in his mind. There were others: men, women, along with the rats and the thickness of the cockroaches. Sometimes he managed to steal a household cleanser. He would use it to encircle the pile of dirty clothes he called home. The goal was to keep the vermin off him. This allowed him to gain some peace that came with short intervals of sleep.

Andy's childhood was one of privilege, travel, private schools, and summer camps. Although everything in the world was going for him, he'd never felt like he fit in. At the time, confusion and a feeling of being not good enough were his norm. At age 13, Andy thought he'd found what he'd been missing all along: a way to fit in and feel like the other kids. He began using drugs and alcohol. He describes it as "being like a raindrop that just fell into a river. Finally, I felt like I was part of it all."

For those who don't understand how a kid with all this going for him can feel that way, consider this: It's a feeling of total isolation in a crowded room. The person sees and hears the other people, many of whom are their friends. They hear the conversations and sometimes are drawn into them but rarely engage.

The thought that rolls around in their mind is, "Why can't I be like the other people?" They wish they were someone else because they think everyone else is better than they are.

Andy had an interest in food and began a cooking career at age 14. He worked as a cook during the summer, as well as after school. Andy was getting high and drunk as much as he could. He attended The Dalton School in Manhattan and graduated from Vassar College.As he matured, his interest in food blossomed, as did his use of mind-altering substances.

Andy spent some time abroad studying his craft. He worked hard and took different jobs as a line chef, sous chef, etc. He studied long hours under some of the best chefs in New York. Although he was getting high and drinking daily, his passion for the food scene never wavered.

Andy sought advice and counsel from successful restaurant owners. He developed relationships with vendors and suppliers. He wanted to know everything: where the freshest fish was coming from, who supplied the best beef, and what foods were trending. He wanted to know who was looking to finance upstarts. He began building strong alliances in the New York food world.

Andy had the drive to succeed in the food industry. It became clear that Andy was extremely talented. He started cooking at high-end and world-renowned restaurants all over New York. All were owned and operated by the superstars of the culinary universe. He helped open and run a dozen restaurants throughout the city. Investing, growing, and building were his passions in those days, along with over-the-top partying.

Andy lied to himself, convincing himself that partying was just part of it. He was rubbing shoulders with the movers and shakers. He was at all the high-end restaurant owners' parties, always telling himself that he was working the system.

Andy's life began its spiral toward the dark hole of the lost. Everyone lives in a small town, even if it's New York City. He would miss meetings or show up drunk. He would disappear for days at a time. His reputation started rotting away until he ultimately lost everything. His family, friends, and money were all gone. The last thing he gave to his addictions was his self-respect and dignity.

Andy burned all his bridges with the people who had initially set him up in business. As he jumped from one to another, his bridges burst into flames at every leap. Andy could not be trusted.

The dismal and dangerous streets of the dirty side of town became his home. Andy ran wild and with the fury of a madman and he lost all sense of right and wrong.

Andy stole, he lied, he connived, he did whatever it took to satisfy his lust for more drugs and alcohol. The feeling of being totally lost was ever present. "What next?" dominated his thoughts and always led to some scheme.

Andy started stealing purses from the backs of chairs while unsuspecting victims dined at their favorite outdoor bistros. He was good at it. Running blind after the deed was done, he would go to the closest place he knew to sell the credit cards and anything else of value. Andy's reward for these acts was to merely survive another day, drugged, lost, and headed toward the hell of running out again.

This lifestyle went on for over a year and a half. Andy's health and his mind rapidly deteriorated. He wasn't the same man who had partied with the elite.

Trying to drink himself to death and feeling like he couldn't even get that selfish act right, Andy reached out to a friend. Once his friend had arrived, Andy immediately tried to talk him out of getting him the help he so desperately needed. Andy didn't want to give up on the notion that he didn't need anyone's help to quit.

Andy tried to get well. He was in and out of numerous recovery programs and attended meetings. Sometimes he could make it three days in a row. Other times, only five minutes after a meeting, he would melt down and use. That was it; Andy had truly lost it all. The once-brilliant and promising young man had hit his bottom.

Andy's big breakthrough happened at the Betty Ford Hazelton Center in Minnesota. There, he was in a 12-step meeting when someone read the promises written in the Big Book of Alcoholics Anonymous. The promises state that you will find a new freedom and a new happiness if you work for it. This time, the miracle happened; the words recited during that meeting took hold in Andy's mind.

Andy finally felt worthy and began his climb out of the depths of addiction. He mounted a full-fledged attack on the addiction that had tortured him for over 15 years. Slowly but surely, the God of the universe began to get his lost child back.

The process of recovery feels grueling and impossible at first. Andy had many setbacks during his earliest stages of recovery. Not relapses of using drugs or alcohol but setbacks involving emotions and time frames. He had accumulated years of hurt and disappointments that took time to heal.

Andy did recover. You will probably recognize the name of Andrew Zimmern. Yes, Andrew Zimmern, TV star and host of the Travel Channel programs "Bizarre Foods," "Bizarre Foods: Delicious Destinations," and "Bizarre Foods America." He is also established and recognized for his writings as a food critic.

Andrew has received four James Beard Awards, one of the highest honors a person can receive in the food industry.

He is happily married to his soul mate and has a son. Andrew will be the first to tell you that he never saw it coming. He never could have fathomed that someday he would have a loving family and the opportunity to entertain the world by sampling the planet's strangest and most exotic foods.

116

Andrew is kind and respectful of other cultures, their foods, their faith, and what they have contributed to the world. His pure joy and happiness are apparent when you watch his programs.

Andrew knows in his faith-filled heart that drugs or alcohol could never replace the peace he has today. His family is sacred to him. He has a morning ritual that includes sliding out of bed and going straight to his knees. He seeks guidance from his power greater than himself. This is a true attitude of gratitude.

Andrew changed his life. He got off the bench, stepped up to the plate of what seemed impossible, swung as hard as he could, and hit his destiny all the way around the world.

Even after getting his life back and achieving so much, Andrew is still very active in the recovery community and speaks freely about his past. He spends time encouraging others, helping them realize that anything is possible in recovery. His webpage, www.andrewzimmern.com, has clickable links to recovery resources for all who seek the freedom of recovery.

For the addicted, getting back family and friends takes time. People in recovery must remember that their loved ones have heard "I will stop" a hundred times. They have heard "I'm sorry" so many times, the phrase means nothing. Those who love the addicted have had their hearts torn out many times. It took a number of years before Andrew's father started letting bits and pieces of his son back into his life.

Andrew knows that when he did what we did, he left an empty spot in others' hearts. They all want that empty spot filled with love for you again. I have listened to Andrew's recovery stories many times in many different formats. Andrew stepped into freedom by applying a 12-step method of recovery. He followed the steps and now is living the promises. This man's story is remarkable.

I have based this story from many public media sources. For more information about Andrews story search the web. Thank you

CHAPTER SIX

THE DIFFERENCE MAKERS

PART TWO

BONES

Nathan Bones, who goes by Bones to his friends, describes it like this: a dull thud followed by a plop. The sound is like dead weight hitting a concrete floor because it is. In prison, there is a constant buzz or hum. It never stops, even at night. It's a sound that is always negative and it weighs on the soul. The sound seems to be carried on an invisible electric wire, humming, lower at times, but always oscillating.

The sound of a dull thud followed by a plop is the sound of an inmate jumping to his death from five levels up, and it makes the invisible wire scream. That sound also makes another sound, a silent one: the sound of hopelessness. Bones went to prison four times.

Bones claims that he was an alcoholic before he ever picked up his first drink. He was at the bar with his alcoholic mother daily. Bones states, "I literally grew up in a bar. I picked up the mannerisms of the drunks at the bar. I listened to their jargon and the way they talked. I was a dry drunk when I was 10 years old because my thoughts were theirs. I was filled with everything negative in the world and this is where I learned to blame everything wrong in my life on someone else."

Bones stole his first taste of alcohol from his mother. At age 12, he and his cousin drank a liquor called Everclear. It has the highest level of alcohol that is legal in the United States. It's pure grain alcohol. Bones ended up hopelessly drunk for the first time in his life and his cousin ended up in the hospital from alcohol poisoning, clinging to life. Bones' cousin did recover, but that experience didn't slow down Bones at all.

"When I was in school, I was labeled as a disturbance. I went through most of my schooling in a juvenile home. I was more than a disturbance, I was a thief," Bones explains. "The reason I was doing all this stealing was to get money for alcohol and for marijuana. I got drunk and high at every opportunity. I loved the effects alcohol and pot had on me. I did my first bit in 'juvie' for stealing bikes." Bones would go to juvenile hall a total of 12 times. At age 16, Bones was caught breaking into a car. He spent the next year in juvenile detention and at the age of 17, he was sentenced as an adult.

Because of his history, Bones received a two- to five-year sentence and went to adult prison for the first time. Near the end of his time inside, Bones became involved in a dispute over one of his shirts. A gang member had taken it and Bones had asked for it back. That gang member told Bones that the minute he walked out of his cell, he would be murdered. Bones looked into the eyes of his potential killer and knew that he was dead serious. Bones got down on his knees and begged God to save him. At that exact moment, Bones heard his name over the loudspeaker. He was escorted to the office and told that he was being released immediately. This wouldn't be the first time the God of Bones' understanding would step into Bones' life.

Under his parole terms, Bones wasn't allowed to be around or consume drugs or alcohol. Unfortunately, Bones wouldn't follow the rules and took up partying immediately, this time at a whole new level.

Bones explains what it was like when he snorted cocaine for the first time. "It was a great feeling when I snorted cocaine for the first time. I could not believe how good it made me feel. However, it went from a good time to becoming the purpose of my life. I would do anything to get it. I would lie, steal, or do whatever it took. It went from a good time to me being found unconscious in the Burger King drive through." Cocaine had complete control over Bones' already troubled life.

Cocaine use became a crack cocaine addiction almost immediately. Bones ended up involved in a check-writing scam as well as possessing large amounts of crack cocaine. One night, Bones and his girlfriend were shacked up in a run-down motel room. Out of nowhere, the door was bashed in and the local anti-drug squad came crashing through. Bones tried to throw the crack into the toilet but openly admits he didn't because somehow he just couldn't flush that much crack down a toilet. Bones caught a one- to six-year sentence in the penitentiary and did a year before being released.

Bones was late coming home one night and his girlfriend was angry. They argued. They'd been staying with his aunt, so Bones grabbed her car keys and took off. His girlfriend called the police and reported the car stolen. Bones was promptly pulled over. Unknown to Bones, his aunt had hidden a handgun in the trunk. The police found it and arrested Bones immediately. Bones was now a felon on parole with a handgun in his possession. He was sent back to prison to finish the rest of his six years.

Bones states that those were some of the best years of his life. The first of the many blessings that Bones would receive in prison was the five-year stay got him off drugs. Bones left the drugs and his tattered life behind him and kept the God whom he had begged to save his life. He started going to church inside the prison and to seek the comfort of God. Bones began serving in the church any way he could. He had become a servant of the God of his understanding. He was humble and non-judgmental, and after two years of service, he was made pastor of the church. He was the leader of the elders of the church and in charge of all the Christian activities in the prison.

When he left prison, Bones was spiritually fit but not suited to live in the outside world. He was lonely, confused, and lost as to what to do with his life. It was only a few short months before Bones was back running with the same drug-addicted crowd. "The gun was my third time inside and a third drunk driving offense during this time frame was my fourth." Bones doesn't remember how long he was in for. "I think I did close to two years but it's a blur."

Bones talked about his last time in prison as being the same but somehow different. "It was the first time I cried when I went in. By this time in my life, I had a baby granddaughter whom I knew I wasn't going to get to see for a few years. I think I cried for a week over that. I felt like there was hope for me and I made up my mind that this was the end of me coming to prison."

When Bones got out of prison, he knew he had to change. His first day out, he sought an Alcoholics Anonymous group to join. He didn't really know anyone, but he could feel an unjudgmental love in the air. The people seemed genuine and to care for one another.

Bones states "There was a camping trip put on by this group and I went. I came there knowing no one and I left having found some real friends for the first time in my life." Bones also shared that when he changed the people, places, and things in his life. He had spent his entire life surrounded by people who used drugs and drank alcohol. His saving grace was surrounding himself with people in recovery.

Today, after five years of continuous sobriety, Bones is indeed a changed man. He is a man of tremendous faith and he lives to serve. He is very active in the same AA group and is sought out by people who are new to recovery and who want to share in his hope for a better life. He has started two new groups for people in his hometown. One is a daytime NA meeting.

This new group is for family members of those who are addicted to anything and whose lives have become unmanageable. This includes addictions to sex, overeating, gambling, or anything else that makes their loved ones' lives unmanageable. Although this is for family members, all are welcome. The group shows family members how to use the 12 steps to cope with their loved ones' addictions.

"I was stunned when I saw all the similarities of those addicted to anything," Bones says. "I can help show anyone who suffers from anything addiction-related or otherwise how the 12 steps of recovery can help."

Nathan Bones is the real deal and his life-changing story can inspire us all. When anything in your life becomes unmanageable, isn't it wonderful to know that you can use any 12-step program to lift yourself up and help win your battle. Please refer to and use a 12-step system to overcome your personal adversity.

Bones is currently working with a woman who is trying to quit smoking. She is addicted to nicotine, and every step of addiction recovery is being used to help her win her battle.

DANCING WITH THE DOPE MAN

J and her partner could feel a hundred daggers of unwarranted hatred being thrown at them. J dancing with the dope man surprised no one as there was nothing conservative or conventional about her life. She was independent, rebellious, and refused to try to fit in the usual box. So, when she arrived at the prom with her African American date, all racist eyes were on her.

This event happened almost fifty years ago. In those days, the Detroit area had very distinct lines drawn in the sand and J had just crossed one. The first one to attack crept up from behind her with a mouthful of slurs. She turned just in time to hear the star football player spew his disdain. She lashed out with her rebuttal, with that he hit her breaking her nose and blackening her eyes. But that was just the start, she and her date continued to be beaten by a gang of white students.

Her date was a superstar as well but his claim to fame was that he was a provider of illegal drugs not only at his school but throughout the area. He was J's hero and mentor. However, after that night, he would never speak to her again.

J's childhood was filled with discipline and control. She was not allowed to leave her yard. She was not allowed to have friends over and was to come home directly from school. For someone who never felt like she fit in anywhere, the only sense of normalcy J could get was when she was able to sneak out with friends.

J's high school days were filled with nothing more than connecting with others to buy and sell drugs. She dealt in any drug she could. She would buy weed by the pound. She would buy and distribute acid, mescaline, angel dust and more. J had business savvy, but it was all going in the wrong direction. On many occasions her actions got her sent to the juvenile detention facility for larceny.

At 15 J was running wild in the streets. She got deeper and deeper into the drug trade and that is where she met her first husband.

Heroin was the next to seep into her soul. J was married and had a daughter. J managed to abstain from her use during her pregnancy as she tried to avoid the tragedy of congenital disabilities so common with heroin use. J and her husband were both heroin addicts and were using multiple times a day.

Home alone during the day J tried her best to keep her addiction hidden from her daughter. One day in particular her daughter woke up early. She was told to never to open her mother's bedroom door, so as her tiny voice rang out the words, "I'm hungry" her mother responded, "I will be out in just a minute, honey." Her daughter persisted, and J's tensions and temper were rising. Her daughter had spotted a small opening in the door and managed to poke her head through. J screamed at her so loud the little girl became terrified and began crying and shaking.

J was stunned by her own actions and words. It caused a devasting flashback of her mother's behavior when she was a child. J was out of her mind with sorrow as she recognized the same look in her baby's eyes that she had experienced with her own mother. Her daughter had witnessed her mother sticking a heroin-filled needle in her arm. The only blessing was that her daughter's age sheltered her from what she was actually seeing but, forty years later J's daughter still has memories of the terror of that moment and the fear she felt.

This had a significant effect on J and may have saved her life. J stopped using heroin and turned to a methadone clinic for help. J's husband stopped using as well but switched to alcohol. Not long after, he drank himself to death, dying of liver failure.

Soon afterword J married a man who was very well connected to the Detroit mob. Although he was not a member of the mob, he had close friends that were. The Italian mafia dominated organized crime and the drug trafficking in the Detroit area at that time. J and her husband owned a couple of bars which kept their real business away from home.

Being so well connected gave the newlyweds access to the type of drug distribution in which J had always dreamed of. Climbing her way to the top had always been easy for J, and soon she was one of the main heroin distributors in the area. The distribution of illegal drugs was not as refined then as it is now. Interstate trucking was the safest and easiest way to receive and distribute.

It did not take long before more and more people got involved in the illegal drug trade. Detroit was in mayhem, drug wars between different factions were brutal. People were getting killed or simply came up missing, and no one could be trusted. The RICO act was being touted about as the authorities began to tie things together. Hidden surveillance microphones and cameras were everywhere. People were snitching on each other for amnesty or protective custody.

It was J's turn in the barrel. She was approached by the feds who offered her a deal to rat out her husband. She refused and the walls around her collapsed. In the black of the night the authorities crashed into J's home. Dope and weapons were found. J and her husband had been set up and caught.

J was poked and prodded by the law to give up her husband and his friends. The questioning was relentless. It was the typical scene you have seen on television with two officials questioning a suspect. It is referred to "playing good cop/bad cop" and using scare tactics describing what life inside prison would be for J.

J refused to turn on her husband they charged her. Not only for her crimes but her role in her husband's crimes. The detectives last words to her were, "If you think you are tough let's see if you can handle a tough sentence."

J was sentenced by the feds and by the state. She eventually would spend two years in federal lockup and 18 years in state prison. The state sentence was not just for drug trafficking. During one of her drug transactions, someone was killed, and the penalty for that was added to her state sentence.

Twenty years is a long time, and lots of things had changed when J was released. J remarked, "The times were the only thing that changes on the inside, you don't."

J went into the system when she was 22 and came out at age 43. J was tempted to return to her old lifestyle feeling that was the only thing she could do.

J soon met a man and they went out on a date. J showed him a stash of cocaine she had. He would have none of it, he took the coke and flushed it. His next moved shocked J as he began to talk about God. J started to go to church and she enjoyed it. J remarked, "I ended up losing the guy, but I kept the God." All through her attempts at recovery she felt there was always a part missing. That part was God.

J was determined now, she started back to school to get her GED, but she didn't stop there. J went on to college and received her Master's Degree in clinical social work. She began her career in the year 2000 as an addiction counselor and has never looked back.

J never sat on the bench. Her life was changed forever by the God of her understanding. J stepped up to the plate of education, took a big swing and hit the ball hard into the entire recovery community.

J started her formal education when she was 43. Can you see that it is never too late? People can come up with a million reasons why this would never work for us. Take a moment and try to find one reason why it will work for you. Use a twelve-step program. J did and now a living miracle walks among us helping hundreds as she goes by.

BIG GIRLS DON'T CRY

B&B's affair had come full circle. She left her husband and their home with a baby swaying on her hip and five bucks in her pocket. Her first stop was the liquor store. With a six-pack in hand, she waited for her new man and her new life to come home from work. They married within a few days of her divorce being final.

B&B lived with her new husband and children out in the country and she felt isolated. With her husband at work, she felt trapped and alone. She stayed drunk all day and was heavy-handed and rough on their two young children. Not unlike other alcoholics, B&B had an internal and unexplainable rage. It circulated throughout her body and mind with every beat of her heart. It lived just below her skin and became electrified with every swallow of her beer. It sparked into a full fury if one of the children acted out. A hard and deliberate smack to the mouth could heard as B&B doled out her immediate sentence. Her alcohol filled mind lied to her and told her it was discipline, when, in fact, it was outrage.

To escape her self-made prison, B&B convinced her husband to let her get a part-time job at night. Reluctantly, her husband agreed with the understanding that she would come home immediately after work. Her dreams had come true, she went to work as a bartender.

B&B and her husband's agreement meant nothing when a good looking and slow-talking cowboy used his sweet southern drawl to urge B&B into his truck. By the end of her first week, she had never come home on time after work. On her last night at work, she met a trucker. He was willing to buy her drinks and he ended up sitting next to her saying all the right things. B&B was playing along with his chatter when she looked down at her half-full beer and said to herself, "What am I doing?" The trucker induced sexual lust that had been running through her mind was suddenly jolted. "I have a husband and two kids at home." With that, she left her last drink of alcohol sitting on the bar.

With tears in her frightened and guilt filled eyes, she arrived at home and was met at the front door by her husband. "I'm afraid for you." He said with a tear of his own. "I'm afraid for me too, said B&B, I can't stop drinking."

B&B has now achieved years of continuous sobriety. Over the course of time B&B struggled to understand why she had become an alcoholic.

B&B shares what she thinks may have been the genesis of her struggle.

B&B thinks this is how it all started. B&B remembers the day that she stared into

her mother's swollen and glassy eyes. They stood out and reflected her blushed tear-streaked face. She looked haggard and worn down. She looked like a woman who had been crying for two days. In fact, she had.

Her mother had left with her father a few days earlier but had returned home without him. B&B was a real daddy's girl and had enjoyed all the perks of having a kind father. She received his gentle hugs to soothe a little girl's troubles, as well as the tickles that generated her giggles.

B&B's father was never coming home. At age forty he died from liver failure as a result of his alcoholism.

B&B was devasted. At six years old she could not understand what had happened. She needed someone to explain to her what had transpired but that explanation never came. He was gone and was never coming back, and that was the end of it. She, her mother and her two siblings simply moved on. It was not acceptable to bring up his passing. It was never talked about or discussed. It wouldn't be until years later B&B would come to understand what the term, "abandonment issues" meant.

The night B&B returned home and admitted to her husband she was scared for herself was a tipping point for B&B. She didn't know where to turn when she finally admitted to herself and to her husband that she had a problem. The next morning, she called the toll-free number for Alcoholics Anonymous and began to create a new life.

Several women from AA took B&B under their wing. They drove her to numerous meetings and soon to meetings all over the state. She attended meeting after meeting, she became "Miss AA." She was on fire. She went back to school and got a degree in addiction counseling. She began teaching classes and living a life of recovery.

B&B was riding high, on top of the charts. She knew what was wrong with other people's paths and she told them so, even if her advice wasn't asked for.

B&B's ego had burst into the sunlight like a giant beam of infinite knowledge. She was full of herself and walking with her head held high, a position her head hadn't seen in a long time.

All felt right with the world until out of nowhere B&B had an awakening of sorts. She was teaching a genealogy class about how alcoholism runs in families. She saw her own background clearly and could not figure out why she had become an alcoholic. She started asking herself again and again, "Why me, since only her father and old Uncle Joe had been what was referred to in those days as "drunks." This haunted her until she could stand no more and for the first time in a long time, B&B had a mental break down.

At work, B&B began to show signs of mental strain and depression. She was not herself, and others took notice. Her boss called her into the office for a talk. After a brief discussion, her boss informed her that she was not to return to work until she met with a therapist he called the dragon lady. It is unclear how she acquired that nickname, perhaps it was because she had a talent for dragging out the truth and for dragging her patients back into reality.

B&B started going to therapy and she began to take an honest look at herself. B&B was indeed suffering from "abandonment issues." The death of her father and the lack of her being able to grieve correctly were creating the problem.

B&B dug in her heels and did the work. She took her therapy to heart and was committed to learning to help herself. This took time, years in fact. R&B learned that her core problem was the feeling of being abandoned. When her father died, she was never allowed to grieve correctly. She was told that big girls don't cry and, if she did, she would upset everyone else for no reason. B&B looked backward in her life to try to understand her choices and her behavior when she entered adulthood. Her training allowed her to see her patterns through-out her life. B&B now understands her struggles.

B&B is an alcoholic in long-term recovery, at the time of this story she had been sober for thirty-six years. B&B had other issues, she freely admits she is an obsessive-compulsive person. At one time in her life, she obsessed with food and tried to eat herself to death. She fought off a compulsion to gamble among other things. She struggled to do anything in moderation.

B&B has used her understanding of a twelve step program to overcome all these issues in her life. Although she admits she is not perfect, look at all she has done. She has incorporated a 12-step program in her life.

Step 1. B&B admitted she was powerless over alcohol, food, gambling, etc. and that her life had become unmanageable.

Step 2. She came to believe that a power greater than herself could restore her to sanity.

Step 3. She made a decision to turn her will and her life over to the care of God as she understands him.

Step 4. She made a searching and fearless inventory of herself.

Step 5. She admitted to God, to herself, and to another human being the exact nature of her wrongs.

Step 6. She became entirely ready for God to remove these defects.

Step 7. She has humbly asked the God of her understanding to remove her shortcomings.

Step 8. She did make a list of all persons she had harmed and became willing to make amends to them all.

Step 9. She made direct amends to the people she had harmed by her actions. She did not make direct amends to those who would have been harmed by her doing so.

Step 10. She continues to this day to take a personal inventory and when she is wrong promptly admits it.

Step 11. She seeks through prayer and meditation to improve her conscious contact with God.

Step 12. She has had a spiritual awakening as a result of these steps and now carries her message of hope to all those that suffer.

Today B&B is living in the solution. She is a contributor and has helped her fellow man in their struggles. She gives everyone a sense of hope when she shares her stories. She is still involved in her local AA chapter and attends regularly.

She has known a new freedom and a new happiness. She has shown that happiness can be found by applying any 12-step program of recovery into your life. B&B is a winner and living proof it doesn't matter how you start, it matters how you finish. She is a dear friend, and I admire her greatly.

LOVE AT FIRST PUFF

In the center court of a housing project, KB was trapped. She was guilty and surrounded. Her crime was stealing the dope dealer's dope. All she had left were her wits, and she began talking and pleading for her life. She thought her denial was making some progress until the dope man pressed his gun to her head. This crime was punishable by death, which had become the sentence of choice. KB could feel his rage through the barrel as it twisted tighter against her skull. She awaited the blast that she would never hear as her body hit the ground. Was this it? Would this be her fate?

KB's early childhood was full of strict rules and discipline. Her parents loved her, and they tried to shelter her from anyone or anything that may have threatened her. Of course, this is the right thing to do, but KB hated it.

KB's parents drank socially and had friends over regularly. KB running to the refrigerator to get someone a beer was considered cute and harmless. The little sips that the guest gave her were also considered acceptable. KB didn't mind at all; she got a "funny" feeling in her body that she liked and was soon sneaking full beers. She liked it because it made her feel different. Her rebellious mind took hold very early and would become one of her downfalls in adulthood.

At age 13, she made up her mind that enough was enough; she would have no more of her parents' discipline. She walked out of her Detroit home and struck out on her own.

"This was the best year and a half of my life," KB remarks with a grin. The dangers of the streets were never an issue for her. She found shelter and safety at every turn. KB took sanctuary with some of the most unlikely surrogates. These were the people of the street, the ones whom society had deemed lost and unsalvageable.

A kind prostitute was the first to take in this always-smiling kid. KB had no explanation for why she offered this kindness. It may have given the woman a sense of hope and an opportunity to contribute something to society. KB never felt like she was in danger and she appreciated the woman's kindness.

One of the next stops on KB's travels was the front door of a well-known drug dealer. He took her in immediately and without an agenda. Divine intervention once again. He never touched her and never left an opening for her to use drugs.

Of course, throughout KB's pursuit of freedom, the law and the truant officer were looking for her. She was caught and given a couple of choices as to her immediate future. She chose the best outcome for herself, which was to move into a home for troubled girls. Eventually, KB was released from the home for troubled girls and given a state-paid apartment.

As a requirement for keeping her housing, KB had to finish high school. Shortly after graduation, she was arrested for the first time, and it was serious. She had committed felony larceny as part of a shoplifting scheme and was sentenced to six months in the county jail.

The day KB got out of jail, she started drinking and using every drug she could get her hands on.

At age 20, KB became pregnant and gave birth to a baby girl. She returned to Detroit to stay with her parents. There, KB ran into old friends who were smoking crack. KB had never smoked crack and it was love at first puff!

Over the next couple of months, KB lost almost 50 pounds and her mother's red flags were jumping up everywhere. KB was running wild in her addiction. Staying gone for days at a time was routine. Her parents now had taken control of KB's daughter and were raising her.

Not unlike most addicts, KB had moments of clarity. During these brief periods of awareness, she was brought to tears, knowing that she should be part of her daughter's life. She could see her baby longing to be held by a mother who was not there. These mental pictures added to the existing layers of shame. KB's shame had become part of her soul and was a major player in KB's downfall.

When KB was 24, her mother passed away. KB was pregnant with her second child. Along with the sorrow of losing her mother, KB now faced a new problem. She was completely addicted to crack cocaine and was clueless as to how she was going to provide for her new baby.

While smoking crack at a drug dealer's house, KB heard a loud voice in her mind. It seemed to come from nowhere, and it screamed so loud at her that she thought others might have heard it. In a clear and decisive voice, the voice yelled, "Run for your life! Get out while you can! Leave Detroit immediately!" KB paid attention and bought a bus ticket. She had ties in a nearby town, which was where she ended up. The power of that voice may have saved KB's life along with the life of her unborn child. That decision to leave would alter KB's destiny.

While she was pregnant, KB slowed her use of everything except alcohol. She gave birth to a healthy son and started putting her life together. She was doing ok at this time and managed to get her four-year-old daughter back. However, the situation didn't last long. After KB gave birth to her third and final child, Child Protective Services got involved. It had leaked out that KB was leaving her kids home alone for extended amounts of time. Crack was back in her life, and it was giving all the orders.

With CPS involved, KB had no choice but to comply. She went to her first recovery treatment center. When she was released, she went right back at it. She believed that crack—not alcohol—was her problem. She attempted to lay off the crack, but eventually, it regained its foothold. This time it took over her life with a new vengeance. It was like the crack had become outraged by its temporary lack of control over her.

Years in and out of rehab, relapse after relapse, the loss of her kids and then getting them back again, occasional homelessness...it was all taking its toll on KB. She would have stints of sobriety and everything would look great...then would come another failure. It was a never-ending haunting and crack cocaine was the ghost. It would leave her alone for a while, then re-appear out of nowhere back into her life. It took on different forms with every new crisis KB manifested in her life.

Then the first of many miracles happened. After leaving her kids and disappearing for three days, KB had an awakening. She knew something had to change. She didn't want to get high anymore. She was given one last chance by a recovery system that she'd always felt was against her.

KB now made a real effort to maintain long-term sobriety. She started doing everything right. KB was going to multiple recovery meetings every day and was involved in her church. She was walking and talking the good news of sobriety and was able to hang onto it for three years this time.

Convinced that she was cured, KB stopped doing everything that had helped her get sober. She spent the next six years up and down, using for a while and then stopping again. At this point in her life, she had been using for years and the consequences were piling up in her thoughts.

One day, while KB was drinking, she had what's referred to as a moment of clarity among alcoholics. No major event happened to convince her to stop. She simply had to decide whether she would continue down this path. She was right in believing that this was more than a God wink. It was the God of the universe reaching for her and touching her soul.

At this point, KB was married to a man she had met in church. KB was almost there in her commitment to stay clean, but not quite. A horrible incident involving her husband and children shattered her world. The details don't need to be shared, but this event resulted in an immediate divorce.

KB was vulnerable, confused, and heartbroken. So, when an old friend showed up at KB's door with a bag of crack, KB gave in. KB was taken in one last time by the monster that had dominated her life for so long. She committed another crime that netted her a thousand dollars. She smoked that up in no time, and she couldn't get high. Her tolerance had been built up for so long that no matter how much she used, getting high was a futile pursuit.

That was that. KB committed the rest of her life to sobriety and swore that she would never use or drink again. KB has been clean and sober for 14 years.

KB turned her life around from a disaster to being a blessing to all she touches. She is admired and respected everywhere she goes. Her counsel is sought daily, and she gives of herself freely.

She got off the bench of the hopeless, stepped up to the plate of a lifelong commitment to God, and hit her blessing as hard as she could, landing in the hearts of everyone who knows her.

KB is a shining example of what is possible in people's lives. She reaches out to others in need at every opportunity. KB is another superstar of addiction recovery.

KB has used the 12-step program to change her life. This is an illustration of what is possible in a person's life when they seek and follow a 12-step program.

CHAPTER SEVEN

THEY OUGHT TO PUT IT IN THE WATER

PART TWO

FIND YOUR PASSION

Laziness, by definition, is slothfulness and a lack of motivation.

I have heard people say, "I'm lazy by nature," and to some degree that is true. If we look back in time, we evolved as hunters and gatherers. If you did nothing to hunt or gather food, you died. The motivation to do the work to save yourself was a real life-or-death situation. Then and now, there are people who will do just enough to get by. There are others for whom just getting by isn't good enough.

My belief is that most people aren't lazy, but they have yet to find what they are passionate about. A clear line can be drawn between someone who is lazy and someone who is perceived as being lazy. In the story below, you will read about a young man who is perceived as lazy, but in reality, he is highly motived.

This young man has worked at a convenience store for years; let's call him BB. BB isn't motivated to contribute more and isn't interested in any part of the convenience store industry. From the outside looking in, he is seen as being lazy. He is a charming young man who is polite and treats the stores customers with respect. However, during idle time, he looks at the clock and can't wait to get off work so he can go to the gym.

BB is a magnificent example of a man who wants to become a bodybuilder. Once at the gym, BB becomes a different person; he is massively motivated. He pumps iron to the point of physical pain. He has a routine and a diet that he sticks to regardless of temptations.

When he's at the gym, BB isn't seen as lazy. In fact, he is looked upon as a superstar who has done the hard work necessary to look the way he does. Although he feels powerful at the gym, he feels guilty at work for not doing more. No matter how hard he tries he just can't "get into it."

BB can't get into it at work because he isn't passionate about what he's doing. Lots of people feel that way; they hate their jobs, but those jobs pay the bills.

What if, in fact, you are a lazy person and you do little to advance yourself? What if your lounge chair is your favorite thing in the house? The television is your entertainment source and is, in fact, a distraction that you use to avoid thinking about how lazy you are. Hope and guidance are available to you; both are illustrated here.

Has this habit of doing very little to advance yourself made your life unmanageable? At work, do you look at the clock constantly? Perhaps you are overweight because you sit around a lot. Perhaps your diet consists primarily of snack foods eaten when you are in your favorite chair.

Here is a call to action! Put this book down and do something immediately. It does not matter how small that action is. Get up and put a glass away. Get up and pick up something that needs picked up! Throw your dirty cloths in the laundry. The point is to take action and to take it in small steps. Do something, anything! Have you ever put something off for so long that it felt like a relief when you finally did it? Why put yourself through the guilt of knowing you need to do something but not doing it? We have all felt that guilt and we have all felt the pain of putting things off.

You can use the 12 steps of any recovery program to overcome this habit that has become your lifestyle. A great way to start is to recognize that this isn't who you are. You are not a habit. The laziness is a symptom of this habit. People who are sick are not their disease. If you are lazy, you are not your bad habit. Don't be defined by what is perceived as a personal shortcoming. Take action, put any 12-step recovery program to work immediately!

Step one of most 12-step programs states that you must admit that, for the moment, you are powerless over this area of your life. If you are powerless over something that you can change then this portion of your life has become unmanageable.

Use step two. Find a higher power. For many, this higher power is God. If that doesn't work for you, find a group of highly motivated people who are doing what you want to do. Regard their knowledge and their drive as a power greater than yourself. Admit to your higher power the exact nature of your problem and become willing to let your higher power help you in your struggles. If your higher power is a group of others, admit to yourself that without help, you are powerless to change.

Come to believe that a power greater than yourself can relieve you of this bad habit. Don't play around with this one. This can and will be life-changing stuff that will have a positive effect on you as well as your family. Humble yourself and turn this problem over to whatever a higher power means to you.

Use step four of most twelve step programs says something like this. Make a fearless and moral inventory of yourself and feel the pain that this habit has brought into your life. Try to feel the pain of everything in your life that you are missing by sitting around watching TV or playing on your computer. The more pain you feel, the more you will want to make this change.

Use step five and admit to your higher power and to someone who is close to you the exact nature of your short comings. This can be an unbelievable freeing experience to share your short comings out loud.

Use step six and become entirely ready to have your higher power help you to remove these issues in your life. Humble yourself and ask for help.

Use step eight and make a list of all the people that your laziness has affected and vow to do better. You don't have to share this list with anyone, but it's imperative that you physically write it down because it will have a far greater impact on you when you can see it.

Use step nine and make direct amends to those who have been affected by your laziness. This is important because it will free you from the guilt and shame you carry.

Use step ten. Continue to take a personal inventory and when you see a lack of effort on your part, admit it immediately.

Don't spend any time beating yourself up when you come up short of your expectations. Revert back to step ten. More than likely, laziness has become a long-term habit in your life. You will struggle when you are trying to make this change. Stick with it by taking small steps. When you see a little thing that must be done, do it immediately. You will instantly get a gratifying feeling. Start from there and build on it.

Use step twelve and be a change maker. Now that you no longer have this bad habit, be an example to others. Show your family members the new you by doing what you say you will do.

Commit to making the change and who knows where it will take you. Perhaps you will become so committed, you will write a book.

LOSE CONTROL

Many of us are burdened by the need to control everyone and everything we can. When I say "burdened," I mean burdened by the weight of the need to control everyone and everything around us. Control is expensive in many ways, but one of the most expensive ways is energy. The constant thought process that says "Listen to me, I'm right" or "Let me do that, you don't know what you're doing" has a very low return on investment and is a massive personal energy leak.

First, to change the desire to control things, the person involved will have to admit that they have a problem. This is defined by the phrase: "You know you have a control problem when your need to control people and things around you causes you problems." Are people frustrated continuously with you? Do you butt into conversations and almost always get a negative response? Are you an overbearing person that must make their point even when it's not asked for? This type of behavior is often a symptom of a root problem, low self-esteem, etc. Often these people are trying desperately to feel accepted.

Lack of feeling accepted is a very serious problem. There can be multiple issues causing this. I am not a mental health care professional. If you think that you have a problem, I would recommend that you seek professional advice. I do know that most of the stories in this book talk about those who have tried to find a place where they feel accepted. Unfortunately, most used people or groups involved with drugs and alcohol to try to feel accepted and fell into addiction because of it.

So, you can see how this behavior can be dangerous. If you are the type of person, who is in constant turmoil with others around you the twelve-steps of most addiction recovery programs may offer you some answers.

Step one of many recovery programs asks you to admit you are powerless over some behavior and because of it a part of your life has become unmanageable. If you cannot stop yourself from the behaviors listed above, then you are indeed powerless over those behaviors. If you struggle with relationships due to this behavior, then this part of your life is unmanageable.

Step two ask you to believe that a power greater than yourself could relieve you from negative behavior. For many people, a power greater than themselves is a God of, "their understanding." If you want to overcome this issue in your life than I urge you to find a power greater than yourself. If not God then perhaps a mental health care professional that is an expert in this area. To change this part of your life, you will have to become humble. You will have to leave your ego at the door so to speak.

Step three states that we must turn our will and our lives over to the power greater than ourselves. For many, this is simply turning their will over to the God of their understanding. Turning away from your ego here is paramount for your success.

Step four ask that you make a fearless and moral inventory of yourself. The people that win and are actually changing their behavior are all capable of being totally honest with themselves. Changing the way you think about things and how you react to things is an inside job. Get honest with yourself, after all, you are the one who has created this problem in your life. Do not spend any time beating yourself up over past behaviors. You are taking action required to change. You are doing what most people with control issues won't do, you have admitted you have a problem, and you want to change.

Step five states that you should admit to your higher power, to yourself, and to another human being the exact nature of your wrongs. Be fearless here and follow these suggestions. You know who you have hurt. Humble yourself and reach out to these people. This very action may ensure that you will succeed. It's an actual honest connection between you and the truth.

Step six states that you must be entirely ready to have your higher power remove your shortcomings. When people get enough pain from their behavior, they will always be ready for a change.

Step seven states that you humbly ask your higher power to remove your shortcomings. Has your behavior caused enough damage in your life? If so, then become ready for your shortcomings to be removed.

Step eight ask that you make a list of all people you have harmed and that you become willing to make amends to them all. This step asked you if you are willing to do this. Willing is the key word here.

Step nine states to make direct amends to such people wherever possible, except to do so would injure them or others. Please use common sense here. It will do no one any good to open an old wound. However, if you are compelled to make something right with someone then do it. Making amends to your family and friends is a powerful healing tool. Once again this will require you to leave your ego at the door.

Step ten ask that you continue to take a personal inventory of yourself and when you are wrong promptly admit it. Most of you have developed this control problem over the course of a lifetime. You will make mistakes and fall short at times in your journey. No, this and take-action immediately when you fall short.

Step eleven ask that you seek through prayer and meditation to improve your conscious contact with your higher power. Reach out into the universe and increase your connections with everything. Being kind to others is something absolute. You will receive more kindness back into your life as you start to improve yourself. When you begin to gain more kindness in your life, and your outlook on your life will change. You will begin to see how important the work that you have done to improve yourself really is.

Step twelve states that you will receive a spiritual awakening as a result of implementing these steps into your life. You will feel like a new person. You will be able to share your knowledge with others, but this time your experience will be sought by others as they see the change in you.

RE-TRAIN Y OUR BRAIN

Negative thinking is a genuine issue for many people. For some, this habit has been ingrained into their thinking for so long it has become their second nature. If you are interested in changing this habit using a 12-step recovery program may help you.

First, think about anyone who has become successful at anything. This could be from the drunk sleeping behind the dumpster who got up and got sober and then went on to become a person of integrity. Or, the guy who worked in a machine shop and went on to become the company's owner. These people think the same way. These people both made a decision to become who they are. These people thought it was possible and they took action every day to make it happen.

These people thought their way into their success. They woke up every day with thoughts of how they could work toward their dream. They formed this habit, and it made them who they are.

If we look at the professional athletes who have achieved their dreams, it would be foolish to think that they did it by pure talent alone. They wake up every day and think about how to make themselves better at what they do. They find a way to take action and improve themselves. A lot of talented people are stymied by the way they think.

If you think that something is holding you back, maybe you're thinking about it the wrong way. I recently had a conversation with a woman who, over a 20-year time frame, generated 15 million dollars.

Through some bad breaks and poor decision-making, she managed to lose everything and is now living month to month in a subsidized housing project. She contacted me on a whim after reading one of my Instagram posts. We eventually managed to talk on the phone, and she laid out her long sob story of all the bad things that had happened to her.

I asked her how much time of her day she spent thinking about her past mistakes and telling other people about how bad she's got it. I wasn't at all surprised about her answer: "I spend all day thinking about it and posting on social media about how hard my life has become." She is not living the life of a person who created 15 million dollars.

Circular thinking happens when a person is experiencing multiple weighty life events. It creates overwhelm in your mind by never slowing down; as soon as one negative thought leaves, another instantly replaces it. Nothing ever feels resolved because these people's brains don't slow down long enough to solve anything. They achieve nothing because they feel like they are powerless to stop it...and at this point, they are correct.

The woman who called me is living in the past. She is spending her time recalling all the events that led to her being broke. She has been doing this for so long, it has become a habit. She is doing the same thing that the people in this article—those who are winning—are doing. However, their thoughts are positive. She wakes up every morning and starts her ritual of reliving the past.

She is getting the same results as the people who are winning. She is getting exactly what she thinks about constantly. She has done this daily for over two years and can't figure out why her life isn't working.

I said to her what I'm about to tell you: "It will never change until you change it, and you change it by taking action." A person can change their thinking by taking charge of their thoughts and holding themselves accountable. It has been said, and it's true, that you can't control the first thought that comes into your mind, but you can control the second thought.

Here's what has helped me stop a negative sequence of thoughts. First, I recognize it immediately. I don't try to stop it by thinking about something positive. That has never worked for me. I stop the thoughts by yelling to myself, "STOP." That immediately disrupts my thoughts. I do this because it instantly puts me back in charge. When it starts again, I yell "STOP" again. If you do this, your ability to control your thoughts greatly increases. It's like building a muscle at the gym; you don't see the results immediately, but with every curl, your muscle gets a little stronger. The same is true with your brain. You are retraining your brain with every "STOP."

Use the steps of any 12-step recovery program, they work! Recognizing that you have a problem is a great achievement! You have just read what has worked for me and now you can try it. Something in your DNA drives you to want to do better. You bought this book, didn't you? Use the steps, admit that you are powerless, and you too will become powerful.

What we all should know by now is this, just because a thought comes into your mind doesn't mean you have to dwell on it and give it power over you. Your mind is like a door that you can open and close at will. With practice and patience, you will begin to choose your focus. You can swing the door any way you would like. Why not focus on thoughts that empower you and allow you to reach the next level in your life? If you choose to focus on the positive every chance you get, you will become a more positive person, and you will draw the right people into your life. Action creates the change and the return on the investment is incredible.

Step one of most twelve-step addiction programs tells you to admit that you are powerless over something. In this case, it's the way you think, and because of this, you are not living a positive life. Then admit that because of this problem, you cannot manage your life the way you would like. Think about that for a second. If you were managing life for someone else how good of a job would you be doing? Would you get a raise, or would you get fired? If you are not winning the way you want to then this part of your life is unmanageable.

Step two says, come to believe that a power greater than yourself can relieve this problem. A power greater than yourself can be the God of your understanding. It can be your willingness to refrain from being around negative people and instead committing to being around people who have winning and positive attitudes. Simply put, change your tribe and you change your vibe.

Step three asks you to turn your will and your life over to the care of God as you understand him. For many people, this works wonderfully. If this doesn't work for you, then recognize that your self-will got you where you are. You must leave your ego out of this equation to succeed. You must find a way. Perhaps it is a group of people who are involved in local positive things and are problem solvers. These type people are only interested in talking about solutions not reliving the same problem over again. I am a member of Toastmasters International, and it attracts people who are upbeat and winning. Look for a Toastmasters group in your area.

Steps four ask you to take a fearless and moral inventory of yourself. Admit to yourself the exact nature of your shortcomings. Stop looking outside for answers. The answer is within you. Take a hard look inside yourself and be honest. You know where you are succeeding and what you need to work on.

Step five asks you to admit to God, to yourself, and to another human being the exact nature of your wrongs. Before anything changes being open about this area of your life is imperative. Admitting to the God of your understanding is self-explanatory. Admitting to yourself what you know to be true is mandatory. In this instance, another human being could be a close friend, your spouse, or someone significant in your life. These people already know you have an issue with being negative. They may have never brought it up, but they know. They will be relieved and happy when you tell them that you are seriously working on this part of your life. This change in your life is a work in progress. Explain to them that you are trying and that you will not always be at the top of your game.

Step six asks that you become entirely ready to have the God of your understanding remove this defect of character from your life. Find a way to make this step work for you regardless of your beliefs. It is a staging area for this change in your life, you must be ready.

Step seven asks that you humbly ask the God of your understanding to remove this shortcoming in your life. The key word here is humbly. You will not succeed in your quest to stop being a negative person without becoming humble. I have had people approach me and ask me how to stop being a negative person. When I tell them to use a twelve-step program of their choice, they sometimes respond, "That stuff won't work for me." I then reply, "So what your doing now is?" Their response of, "that stuff won't work for me" is a negative response. That is not a humble approach to the issue. Better said would be, "I don't know how to stop being negative, and I'm open to anything that might help me." Humble yourself, and you will succeed.

Step eight asks you to make a list of all persons you have harmed due to your behavior and to be willing to make amends to them all. This is simple, are you willing to make amends?

Step nine asks you to make direct amends to such people wherever possible except when to do so would injure them or others. Do not overthink or over-respond to this. Keep it simple. Talk to your loved ones and tell them you are sorry for responding negatively to them and their opinions or ideas. This is humility in action.

Step ten is to continue taking a personal inventory and admit when you are wrong. You must remain committed. Look at your daily actions. Are your daily activities leading you to the life you want to live? If you ignore this, you will slip back into your old habits. It's not that you are a terrible person or a failure. It's human nature, so continuously be aware of your thoughts and actions.

Step eleven asks you to improve your conscious contact with the God of your understanding. Meditate on your willingness to let go of the old you. Ask for the knowledge to continuously grow and do better. All of this will keep you connected to living in the solution regardless of your beliefs. You are already living in the solution, you are reading these steps and raising your awareness.

Step twelve states that you will have an awakening of some kind and as a result of this awakening you will be willing and able to have a positive impact on those around you.

This program of success works if you work it. It will keep you in the solution. Know that negative thinking is a pattern and a habit that will fight you. That doesn't mean that you are a bad person. It means you are human. Change comes slowly at first in anything. The more you feed yourself with positive thoughts that lead to solutions the more momentum you will gain, and before you know it, you will be living your life in a beautiful positive way.

CHAPTER EIGHT

THE DIFFERENCE MAKERS

PART THREE

BLACKOUT TO BREAKTHROUGH

At age 13, C got drunk at a Quinceanera. A Quinceanera is a time-honored Catholic custom and celebrated by factions of the Hispanic community. It occurs on a girl's 15th birthday.

The celebration began and the black ties and formal gowns were all about when C was offered her first drink of alcohol. She tasted the champagne and liked it. Then she downed all of it. Before the night was over, C was so drunk, she caused multiple humiliating scenes. She had ruined this glorious event for everyone and had destroyed the guest of honor's special day.

C didn't drink again until she was a senior in high school. She went to a party and wanted to be like the others there. She wanted to drink and have fun like everyone else, but she couldn't. C always got drunk, blacked out, and caused an uproar. This convinced her that it would be better if she drank by herself. For her, the struggle was real. She suffered from depression due to the loss of all her friends and to her inability to fit in anywhere.

C started experimenting and drinking alone at home. She drank until she found what she describes as "the warm spot" in her body. She would get there, but she could never stop. The good news was that no one from school was there to laugh at her.

C went off to college and a new excitement fell upon her. This was a chance to put everything behind her. It was her chance to start a new life with new friends and new opportunities. She didn't realize that changing real estate never helps. C was bringing the same problems to a new place.

When C arrived on campus, everything went well for a time. She went to a few parties that served beer. She didn't like beer, so she would nurse a few of them, and everything worked out fine.

The first weekend C was home, her parents went out for the evening. As soon as they were gone, she attacked their liquor cabinet. When C drank, she wanted to go to a happy place in her mind. However, no matter what, the alcohol never took her there.

Sometime before her customary blackout, she called friends and told them that she was going to take her own life. The next thing she remembers was the sound of pounding on the bathroom door. It was the police.

While the rescue personnel were taking her to the ambulance, C heard a sound that is still vivid in her mind today. It was the sound of her dad's troubled voice asking, "Has she been drinking?"

Once at the hospital, C began talking gibberish, which terrified her dad. His usual firm voice now quivered, then turned into a confused sob that he could not hold back. Due to her behavior, C was admitted to the psychiatric ward. This was the first time. There would be six more.

Eventually, C returned to school and decided that it would be better if she lived off campus. Her parents set her up in a small house but her sanity lasted for only about a month before the usual devil's chatter started talking to her mind. C drank herself into more insane behavior.

C's now-familiar pattern of drinking herself into a dark place struck again. Alcohol and too many Tylenol were the reasons for her next trip to the hospital and her second stay in the psychiatric ward.

C's refusal to jump through the necessary hoops to return to school left her alone and depressed again. Her dad quit his long-term job and moved in with her. He begged and pleaded with the doctors and the staff to let C return to school. It all came down to her unwillingness to meet the school's demands and talk to the school psychiatrist. Her dad went back home, his heart broken as he prepared for the next crisis. Shortly after he left, C's next crisis was her first DUI.

Party time was in the air and C began to plan a huge bash for her 20th birthday. She even recruited her aunt to help her set up, plan, and prepare for the party. Lots of booze was purchased in anticipation of the big night. All through the day of the party, C was filled with excitement. At last it was party time. The scheduled start time came and went. As the evening progressed, the sparkle that she'd worn all day began losing its shine. Nobody came. C's already-low self-esteem spread its roots ever deeper as each minute passed. She was devastated. Eventually, four or five people did show up. C struggled not to let her disappointment show on the outside. However, after she swallowed the same pill of self-blame over and over, it turned bitter, and C drank herself into another blackout.

The next three or four days were somewhat cloudy. C stayed drunk from the leftover booze. She doesn't recall the sounds of the sirens or the flash of the multicolored lights or the words of the police officer. She had no idea what time of the day it was, but she knew that being caught driving drunk in her pajamas was inappropriate.

The next day, C's dad came to get her. They went to her parents' house. She recalls sitting on the floor of the living room and telling her overwhelmed dad that she thought she was an alcoholic. Her dad screamed at her, "You ought to be committed." He was at his wit's end and was shaken to the core.

A few weeks before C's 21st birthday, in the middle of one of her blackouts, she cut herself intentionally. At the hospital, she received stitches for her wound and a trip back to the psychiatric ward. This was the third time before she was 21 years old.

That summer, C went completely off the deep end. She was 21 and hitting all the bars. She hooked up with a buddy who was always willing to go for a drink. One time, C's buddy dumped her in public and left her stranded in the bar district. Alone, C stumbled out of one of the bars, fell on her face, and tore her ACL.

The hospital, her dad, returning to school, and then quitting school composed the next set of circumstances in the seemingly never-ending drama that was C's life.

Another car crash while driving drunk earned C another trip to the psychiatric ward. However, things would be much different this time. A mercenary of God walked into the ward. He was a recovering alcoholic volunteer who came to spread the message of hope to anyone who wanted to hear it. It was then when C experienced her first AA meeting. They read a story of success in the big book, and near the end, the volunteer read the promises of AA. The one promise that stuck out in C's mind was "You're going to know a new freedom and a new happiness."

What impressed C the most was the sight of him leaving. He walked out the door a free man, open to do anything in his life but drink. C realized that every time she'd had a major problem in her life, she was drunk.

The next morning, C called her dad and said, "Dad, I think I'm an alcoholic." He reacted and sent out the undying love and compassion that only a parent can know. "Mi Hija" were the next words out of his mouth. This is a common and affectionate term that means "my daughter" in Spanish. "I am so proud of you."

The following week, the same volunteer returned to the hospital and they had a group meeting. It was there that C admitted she had a problem. The next day, a staff counselor approached her and started talking about alcoholism treatment centers. C was now open to the idea that she needed help. She spent 30 days in a Texas facility and then went to a treatment center in California.

C was released from the treatment center and went to the airport. The minute she got there, she started drinking.

The next stop landed C in Arizona to catch a connecting flight. Immediately, she went to the bar. At the airport, a kind police officer picked up on C's drunkenness and despair. He assured her she was going to be ok and took her to the hospital just to be sure.

C returned home as lost as ever. Her dad begged her to go back to AA. That made her go on the defensive and scream, "You don't understand," as she rejected his pleas. As time went on, she met some sober friends and then committed herself to go to AA to appease her parents.

One night, C came home drunk. She became violent and acted crazy. Her parents called the police. C was arrested for domestic violence and went to jail for the night. The next day, she returned home to find a dad who did not know what to do. He just wanted his "Mi Hija" back.

The next semester, C went back to school and met the man who is her husband today. She tried to keep her alcoholism hidden, but what always happens happened: Her husband found out. Once again, through her depression and her behavior, she found herself in the psychiatric ward.

C's husband stood behind her all the way. She agreed to go to a rehab facility in Florida, then one in Texas. Both were filthy and poorly run. C got nothing from either.

C returned home and started drinking again. A week later she was admitted to the psychiatric ward. She was suffering from a deep and relentless depression. A trip to the doctor convinced her to attend a depression clinic, and it seemed to help for a short time. Then, within a few weeks, a friend committed suicide and C drank herself into a blackout state.

Once C came out of it, she sent a crazy text to her mom, talking about hurting herself. When her mom arrived, C was in the bathroom, unconscious on the floor and covered in blood. She had cut her face and was almost dead. C was rushed to the ER. The doctors on staff were not optimistic. She was placed on a ventilator to get her breathing normally again. In the psychiatric ward, her nurses called her by name because she had been there so often.

Upon release, C drank the next week and then the week after. She went to a family event and tried to get just a little drunk. History repeated itself and she caused a big scene, leaving everyone angry and horrified about what she had become.

The day before her last drink, C had run out of alcohol, so she mixed rubbing alcohol with something else (the other element remains unknown) and put the mixture in her purse. C's husband returned home, and she showed him what she had done. He was stunned and tried to explain to her what happens to people who routinely drink these types of concoctions. They end up blind, dead, or permanently brain-damaged.

C's husband left for a while, then returned with a big book of Alcoholics Anonymous. "I think you need this," he said. She opened it and read the promises of recovery. She remembered the man who had come to the psychiatric ward and how he had left free to do anything with his life except drink.

The next 12-step program and recovery center that C visited took root in her mind. She ran into an old friend to whom she could talk. C learned that everyone deserves recovery, no matter their past. Her friend told her to go back to the AA meetings, which she agreed to do.

C attended AA meetings, readings, study groups, and women's meetings. She got a sponsor and grasped hold of everything she could that dealt with recovery. The energy of being surrounded by people just like her was exciting. At last, she had found a place where she fit in. She started attending two or three meetings a day; she was committed.

Today, when C wakes up, she fills her mind with the benefits of recovery. She recognizes that she can do anything! She doesn't have to go to jail. She doesn't have to go to the psychiatric ward. She is free to live a wonderful and blessed life.

C got off the bench, stepped up to the plate of sobriety, swung at it with everything she had, and hit a long fly ball deep into the heart of Texas. She has lived quite a life for a person who was only 29 years old as of the time of this writing. When asked if, a few years ago, she could have believed that this new freedom was real and achievable, she replied, in a tear-filled voice, "No, it is truly a miracle from God."

C has been sober for four years now. She is happily married and is working on her career. She is in the medical field and her potential is limitless.

KATZ DANCE

"I know I am here for a reason." Those were Katz's first words to me at the beginning of our interview. "I have lost so many friends to the needle that I'm sickened by each new Facebook post saying 'RIP.'"

"I have always been able to come out of things, but it was close the night I shot up a friend and he died before my eyes."

The setting was a dimly lit room where a handful of shaky addicts were trying to get their load on. The curtains were drawn to hide them from the light and from unwelcome eyes. They have been called "creatures of the night" in scripture: "Those among us who thrive in the dark." The darkness says more about them than the absence of light does. It speaks of the shadows' need to mingle one among the other without fear of exposure.

The atmosphere in the rooms felt heavy. The vibrations of the karma being cast about made the air thicker. Chairs had been placed around the living room, giving some of the players a place to steady their arms. The furniture was worn and tired from the constant ups and downs required to peek out the window as the spirit of paranoia filled the room.

Katz's friend was no stranger to the needle. His veins were mushy and slid back and forth as if trying to elude the dagger. The paleness of his arm revealed more about him than his chalky off-white color. His constant absence from life's natural sunlight spoke more about his secrets than his skin tone. Katz went to work trapping the vein and leaving it no place to hide. With the thrust of the plunger, her friend felt whole again as the poison took hold. He sighed with relief as the artificial dopamine lied to his brain, giving it a false sense of being ok.

The lie didn't last long. Her friend's body screamed NO as he went into toxic shock. His heart stopped, interrupted by the lie.

His lungs could no longer suck air and his breath died. Cold, pale, and lifeless, he collapsed. Katz came to life at the horror. She began giving him CPR and pumping his chest. "Come on, come on, God help me, don't let him die." The fear of calling the authorities isn't like it was a few short years ago. The law forgives instantly, and 911 was called immediately. Within minutes, the paramedics and the Narcan arrived. The paramedics went to work at a frantic pace. "Hit him again!" the paramedic shouted.

"Nothing."

"Hit him again."

With that, vomit swelled in his mouth. The vomit cleared his throat, leaving room for a breath of hope as he gasped for air. By grace, he was alive but the saving grace didn't stop there.

Katz stood silent save for her trembling lip. The trooper's voice was firm but compassionate as he asked Katz for the truth. Katz admitted to her role; her truth was frightening to tell but it felt freeing. The officer took her to the side and, with calm eyes, told her of the consequences she would have faced had her friend died. He spoke softly, trying to calm her wild and terrified eyes. Second-degree murder, involuntary manslaughter, and delivery of an illegal substance causing death would have been on the table for the county prosecutor to choose from.

Katz's voice quivered as she repeated her opening statement to me. "I've always been able to come out of things," she said, "but it was close that night."

"Pass the joint" isn't something a parent should be saying to their 11-year-old daughter but for Katz it had become the norm. Katz came by her use of drugs and alcohol naturally. Dysfunction comes in many forms and labels and can be confusing to the novice. Katz's family's dysfunction needs no fancy name; it was simply the wrong way for a child to grow up.

The dysfunction of Katz's early youth grew right along with her into high school. The bathroom at school, with its marble floors and sterile lighting, served an additional purpose along with its normal function. "At lunch, the bathroom at school was the place to score drugs," Katz recalled. "If you wanted dope or needed a place to use, the bathroom was the hot spot. You could tell what was happening if you looked under the stall door and saw three sets of legs."

Katz took a breath and paused before continuing. I could feel her looking at her past and seeing the faces of her youth and of her classmates who now resided in the graveyard. "So many gone, and I could have been one of them. I know I'm here for a reason."

Katz has a solidness about her. It's hard to describe; she doesn't carry the presence of a lifelong drug addict. She graduated from high school and went on to graduate from nursing school. Her next remarks made her voice quiver again. "I stole prescription pain pills everywhere I worked. I stole pain pills from my grandmother when she was dying. I'm ashamed of that."

Shame is hard to measure because it lives in so many places within us. It lives in our memories, tucked away but always at the ready to tell us why we don't deserve something better in our lives. It lives in our hearts. We can feel our hearts sink every time we lose out on something due to our past behaviors. The consequences of our past seem to never end. Shame lives in our souls but remains elusive. It's that feeling we get when we are unsettled for no reason. Shame causes relapse after relapse, keeping us from our destiny … and keeping our cemeteries full. Shame is a scourge on mankind.

Katz was now in her 20s and her addiction showed no mercy. Her nursing career was gone due to her drug use. Hanging with the wrong crowd and not feeling worthy, Katz saw an opportunity to earn her much-needed dope money. At this point, she was a full-blown heroin addict, living by the lie, "I'm not a real junkie; I only snort heroin." The strip clubs were always hiring the lost and vulnerable. Katz was both.

Katz danced her way around a few different clubs, changing locations but not really changing anything else. The faces may have been different but the slobber and lust from the crowd were the same. The managers of the places where she worked had different faces as well, but their agenda was the same: money. They watched as these women deteriorated before their eyes. They watched as the kids got taken away, they watched as some died, they watched and took full advantage when one of the dancers was short on dope money and had to do what she had to do. They were there for "their girls" as long as "their girls" were willing to satisfy their handlers' own lust. Some demanded sexual acts that were unspeakable.

All along Katz's path, there had been her boyfriend, whom she had been with since high school. He was as addicted as she was and had no problem with Katz stripping. He was ok with it as long as she brought home enough money to keep him high. However, her family could take no more and told them both, "Either go to treatment or you can't stay here anymore." Both agreed to go to treatment and both were admitted into a long-term treatment facility. Katz hid her dope in a very personal spot to smuggle it in. Her boyfriend hid dope in his hat.

The recovery center offered almost as much dope inside as was available outside. Katz's boyfriend deemed it a joke and left after a few days. Katz hung around for a while but soon followed. They both went back to the family and reported themselves cured. Their naive families saw no reason to question them and they were welcomed back home. They wore out their welcome in short order and were asked to leave.

Treatment center after treatment center, as well as relapse after relapse, was their course for the next few years. Along the way, Katz began thinking that she really did want to quit before fate led her to the same end that so many of her friends had faced. She had been caught shoplifting twice in the same week and during one of the arrests, she was carrying four grams of heroin. She realized that she would never get well with her long-term boyfriend in the picture. This hurt her, and it took some time, but she ended their 14-year relationship.

With a nudge from the judge, Katz entered a long-term treatment center. This time, she took it seriously. She started getting well and learning the coping skills required to live a drug-free, healthy life. Katz is a naturally beautiful woman and attracted the attention of a young man who had taken his recovery seriously as well. They began writing to each other, which led to them spending time together.

It is recommended that a person not enter a personal relationship with anyone who is as new in recovery as they are. My personal recommendation is that you get a house plant. If it's still alive at the end of six months, go ahead and get a puppy. Start from there.

Katz and her newfound love began attending recovery meetings regularly. They were both on the right path, and still are. Somewhere along the way, Katz became pregnant. She was terrified and shared this with me: "I didn't know how to take care of myself yet, let alone a baby." "How was her newfound love going to take the news?" Tears rolled down her cheeks as she shared with me the plan she had laid out. "I wrote him a letter and asked him if he wanted me to keep the baby." Little did he know she had already scheduled an abortion. That letter changed their lives. They agreed to have the baby and are now the proud parents of a beautiful baby boy.

Today, Katz lives in the promises of recovery. She has used the 12 steps and continues to do so to address any issue that life hands her. She recognizes her family's dysfunction when she was young. She knows that she is powerless over her past. She will not take on a victim mentality. Instead, she gets up every morning and puts one foot in front of the other. She is moving toward a promising future for herself and her family. Katz has stepped into a new freedom and has found true and real happiness.

GRANDMA'S GARDEN

A description of a dope house and one woman's trials starts Yvonne's story.

The abandoned needles lay on the floor like tiny pit vipers. They wouldn't hurt you unless you stepped too close or had a misstep avoiding one only to be bitten by another. Yvonne knew the hazards and the danger that lay about. Yet she still coaxed her pregnant daughter to come in with her. The total lack of regard for anyone or anything is a junkie's trademark. She was more than willing to put her pregnant daughter at risk with never a thought to the unborn that lay within her.

Yvonne F's life was affected by alcohol very early on. Her mother and father were both severe alcoholics. The first sign of damage as a result of their alcoholic behavior came when Yvonne was six months old. It was only the beginning and far from the end of the atrocities this child would have to endure. Yvonne never knew anything had happened to her until she was looking thru some old photos with her beloved grandmother. As they casually glanced through the picture's, they came across one of Yvonne as a baby. She had braces on her legs. When she asked her grandmother why she had braces, she could see her grandmother's face change to a look of disgust.

As Yvonne looked into her grandmother's eyes, she could feel the hurt and the burden of keeping this secret hidden for so long. Her grandmother told her that her father did this to her. He had slammed her into a wall because in his mind Yvonne had come along and ruined his perfect little family. He had all the kids he wanted, and she was not one of them. In an alcoholic rage, he took his frustrations out on his baby girl that he wanted nothing to do with let alone raise. The baby's injuries were explained away as an accident at the hospital, and the lie was hidden seemingly forever.

Yvonne's mother divorced her natural father and immediately married another alcoholic. People who are alcoholic tend to follow the same destructive patterns so her mom marrying another drunk was no surprise. Her new stepfather pretended to like his newly acquired stepdaughter, but for all the wrong reasons. Not long after they were married he began to sexually molest Yvonne. The length of time this went on is unknown, but it was over the course of several years.

At age 10 Yvonne started to sneak and drink alcohol. The winds of a life of misery began to blow. Over the course of time, they would turn into a hurricane with every aspect of her life being scattered and strewn.

It has come to light that in many cases of child molestation the victim blames themselves. They begin to live a life of shame and that is why so many of these incidents go unreported. Trying to bury their hurt with drugs and alcohol feels easier and quicker. Using drugs and alcohol acts like a nerve blocker between their brain and the reality of what they have had to endure.

Yvonne's mother continued her same pattern of destructive behavior. She divorced again then and married another alcoholic. This new man that came into Yvonne's life was different than the rest. Even though he was an alcoholic, he showed her the kindness and love that she so desperately needed. He has long since passed, but Yvonne still refers to him as 'daddy.'

Sadly, Yvonne's new stepfather got into the picture too late. She was already far into her alcohol and drug habit. She was sneaking and drinking full time now and had also made a giant leap into hard drugs. PCP was her new drug of choice.

The madness of this kid gone wild could not be stopped. Yvonne wasn't just drifting toward disaster she was sprinting toward it. When a person endures a life that they have no control of from birth to age 16, they truly are a victim. Her young mind never had an opportunity to develop correctly. The next few years of Yvonne's life where a staging area for the trouble that was to come.

Yvonne recalls a bright California day at her grandmothers. The sunshine peeked and trickled thru a lattice. Her grandmother's bird aviary was normally a place of sanctuary for Yvonne from the day to day troubles of her world. It sat peacefully in an isolated place as if it was an oasis in the desert of the hustle and bustle. There was calm there, and one could blend into its greenery and the bird life as if they were part of it all.

Its abundant growth naturally camouflaged Yvonne's presence and gave her an opportunity to find some artificial peace that she could only find in a heroin-filled needle. The fresh prick of the needle left a small stream of blood running down her arm. Her secret task complete, she turned out of her hiding place and ran headlong into her grandmother. Their chance meeting startled them both, and her grandmother was the first to speak, "What are you up to out here?" Her question was asked innocently and without any tone of accusation. Then her grandmother glanced down and noticed the trickle of Yvonne's life blood on her arm. Yvonne's grandmother asked what had happened? Yvonne, replied quickly, as if a fast answer would erase what had already seen, "Nothing grandma, I'm only looking at the birds." Her grandmother looked at her and silently walked away.

Little did Yvonne know that those would be the last words the only true friend she had ever known would ever say to her. Later that afternoon her grandmother went to the hospital complaining of chest pains. Congestive heart failure was the diagnosis, and the woman that had been Yvonne's rock never left the hospital.

A few years later, after a routine surgery, Yvonne's body went haywire. Over the years she had become infected with HEP C which compromised her immune system. She was sickly in her appearance. She lost a massive amount of weight and her hair fell out. Every system in her body turned against her.

Eventually she was released from the hospital and gave her body a brief time out from substance abuse, but that timeout was truly brief. Before long she was off and running again, a run that would continue for seven years.

This insanity only leads in one direction and Yvonne's life was on a fast track to the cemetery. Meth was her drug of choice during this period of madness. She had no idea that God's light was heading her way. In the hospital she had thought "This is it I will never use again." When that happened there was is a crack formed in Yvonne's armor of her addiction, a crack that would eventually break wide open and let in the light of the truth.

Sometime near the end of this seven-year run her daughter (a recovering addict herself) began to text her. She would tell her of one death after the other from snorting crystal meth. Yvonne finally agreed to stop snorting meth. What she didn't tell her daughter was she started shooting it.

Yvonne had started slamming (shooting up) meth into every vein available and the track marks dotted her body. She had damaged her veins so badly that she couldn't find one that she could stick the needle into without it collapsing. Her "friends" were called in to rescue her. Their shaky hands stabbed at one vein after another, often missing their mark causing her to scream in agony. She was in misery and she had had enough.

Yvonne called her daughter and asked if she could move in with her and try to stop this madness. Her daughter agreed, so Yvonne put her belongings into storage and off she went to her daughter's apartment.

The struggle to come down from meth is miserable. Yvonne began her come down with the help of the prescription drug, Adderall. The effects of a withdrawal from methamphetamine are dangerous. She describes it as if she were being shocked. She would be fine, maybe she would be walking in the kitchen for something and bang it was as if she had just stuck her finger into an electrical socket. We have probably all been shocked at one time. When it happens, we withdraw from whatever caused it and its over. Not this, it was like Yvonne was being shocked, and she couldn't get away. Yvonne's body went into spasms that lasted for more than a minute. Her body would begin to convulse, and there is nothing she could do about it.

During this period, her daughter was in early drug addiction recovery herself and had had her children taken away by Child Protective Services. She was committed to stay clean and sober and to get her children back. She was on probation so any involvement with people using drugs or people involved in drugs would put her at risk of violating her probation, and not getting her kids back.

Yvonne's daughter was terrified every time her mother had one of these horrible electrical episodes. Yvonne had about ten-days-worth of Adderall left. Her daughter begged her mother to let her buy a $20.00 bag of meth so that she could come down slowly. Her daughter was willing to risk everything including her sobriety and her kids to help stop the nightmare her mother was going through. Yvonne finally agreed, and the call was made to the dope man. Within a few hours, Yvonne had the little baggy in hand. Over the next ten days by combining the two drugs, Yvonne weaned herself off methamphetamines.

This woman's story is remarkable. Yvonne got off the bench, and by addressing her decades of a life that was so lost she was able to step up to the plate, she swung at forgiveness for the ones that had hurt her so deeply and hit a home run into the parking lot of the forgiven and the redeemed.

Yvonne now is involved in a tremendous amount of recovery based activities and programs. She has worked for and achieved many highly sought accreditations. Her recovery community, as well as the State of California, have recognized her with certifications that only come after hard work and study. She has been honored by her peers and is a name that is recognized in the circles of the recovery community. Yvonne has left the past behind and has become a difference maker in other people's lives.

She admitted that she was powerless and came to believe that a power greater than herself could restore her back to sanity. She worked a twelve-step program for people addicted to drugs and she won.

If something in your life is holding you back won't you try a twelve-step method? It has worked for millions.

SHE USED FOOD

The getaway vehicle was parked in the alley in a pre-determined location. The kidnapping of four innocent children began to unfold in broad daylight. L and her three brothers and were forced into an old van before it raced away, she was 5 years old.

Confused and shaken L's tiny mind had already been through more than any child should have to endure. L was a victim of an unstable home life full of erratic behavior and alcoholism. The filth these children were raised in was an abomination. Their father was an off again on again over the road trucker and a raging alcoholic. Their mother claimed to be a "Go-Go Dancer." But in reality, she was a stripper.

The children were often left to fend for themselves and more times than not with no food in the house. One day, their father was laying on the couch hung over and sick. The house reeked of vomit and filth, but it smelled of another foul odor, the odor of desperation and of addiction. If her parents could have smelled it before it became overwhelming perhaps, they would have tried to stop it.

Dependencies and dysfunctions are a slow process that happens before everyone's eyes. The family and the loved ones smell it first. They smell the rot coming forth in every poor decision that's made. They catch a whiff at every holiday when one of the parents shows up drunk or stoned. They try to weigh in or reach out, but their words are always met with the same disdain, "It's none of your damn business how I raise my kids."

Before anyone realizes it, the children have become secondary. Their parent's addictions outweigh the needs of their children, and the children become second place in their lives.

The neighborhood around the children's home had become increasingly aware of the children's blight. The neighbors had been checking in on the children as often as they thought they should dare, and on this day, they were particularly disgusted. The children's grandmother was contacted, and she alerted Child Protective Services. CPS came immediately and removed the children from the squalor.

Temporarily in their grandparent's custody, their mother somehow learned of their location. Like thieves, she and some friends carefully planned the kidnapping. When the time was right, she swooped down and made her move. Her mother was in a blind rage but managed to get all of the children in the getaway van.

The children were taken to one of her mother's friend's apartment where they were kept out of sight. It may have been few days or maybe a few weeks, L doesn't really remember how long they were held. Perhaps through some investigation or alerted by someone the authorities learned of the whereabouts the children.

The authorities moved in and removed the children. Their mother was never allowed to see her children again without supervision. Their mother made the appropriate arrangements and saw her kids a few times but soon drifted away and disappeared.

L's two older brothers were sent to a boy's youth home. L along with her younger brother were put into foster care and placed with a couple. It was in the care of this couple that L's story gets worse instead of better.

The couple that L and her brother had been placed with were alcoholic and abusive in every way imaginable. From age six until thirteen L suffered daily. Graphic details of what went on while she was in foster care will not be disclosed at the request of L.

Fear and shame were used to intimidate these children. The woman of the house took great pleasure in her threats and lies of what would happen to the children if they ever told anyone what went on at that house. Children this young, are particularly vulnerable to fear-based tactics.

At age thirteen L and the woman were in an argument over some records that were scattered on the floor. L was determined to get to school on time and refused to take the time to clean them up. The woman became enraged and threw a full unopened can of beer at L striking her squarely in the eye. L's eye was swollen shut by the time she got to school.

L's teacher's instinct was a lifesaver. When she questioned L about what had happened to her eye, L told the truth. The authorities were contacted immediately and legal action to remove the children was taken. Later that same day the children were removed from what L describes as, "the house of horrors." The woman involved died three months later of liver failure due to alcoholism.

Much of the time when children like L have spent their entire lives being controlled by someone else in a negative way the need to take control of themselves becomes paramount. When she was in high school L found a way to gain some level of control over herself. Unfortunately, it came in the form of an eating disorder. She began to use food as an object not as nourishment. By controlling what she ate, she could control the way she was looked. Therefore, she thought she could control how other people saw her.

Of course, staying fit looking and eating correctly are positive things, but for L it wasn't like that. She needed to take real power over her life, so she began to binge and purge. Binging and purging are the primary symptoms of Bulimia, the act of eating as much as one can and then immediately vomiting up what was eaten.

L describes what happens to a person when they force purging. There is a chemical and a physical reaction that occurs in a person's body when they purge that feels like they are going to lose consciousness. L reports that she really didn't like the way it felt, but it was better than the way she felt about herself. It became an escape from reality for her, and it became a habit, a nasty habit that continued off and on for years.

L was then and is today a beautiful woman, so it was natural at that time to seek a modeling career. L became so conditioned to the act of binging and purging that she could literally vomit on command.

Because of L's modeling appointments locations she was forced to use busy highways to go to and from her different job's. L recalls driving down a particularly busy stretch of highway in California. Cars were always speeding and darting in and out of the multiple lanes. L frequented this stretch of highway to drive to or from her next modeling appointment. L became so good at her purge that she kept a large plastic container in her car. She could vomit into the tub while driving down the highway dodging in and out of the traffic.

During this time in L's life she added a new addiction, alcohol, resulting in all the usual negative results of alcoholism. She struggled with job loss, relationship problems, money, etc. Her bulimia and her alcoholism had taken their toll on her body and on her life. At the age of twenty-four L told herself enough was enough and she made a decision to stop both.

L entered a twenty-eight-day inpatient facility to address her issues. She looked at the twelve steps of Alcoholics Anonymous and immediately recognized that the same steps that had saved so many alcoholics could be applied to her eating disorders.

(1) She admitted she was powerless of her eating disorders and that her life had become unmanageable.

(2) She came to believe that a power greater than herself could restore her to sanity.

(3) She made a decision to turn her will and her life over to a God of her understanding.

(4) She made a searching and moral inventory of herself.

L was able to overcome her food affliction by using a twelve-step recovery program.

L did well with her alcoholism recovery for a few years. However, she did relapse and was lost for another eight years. Today she has been clean and sober for three years. She has three children and has been married to the same man for nineteen years.

L still deals with some treatable mental issues and some issues from her youth. With the twelve steps deeply ingrained in her she knows she can give back to others and live a happy life. Her hope is that her story will help someone else overcome their personal obstacles.

A MESSAGE FROM GOD

Mike was a good kid who grew up in small-town America. His parents were divorced but his life was relatively stable. Mike was well-liked and popular in school. However, an event in his senior year of high school would change Mike's life forever and could have had grave consequences.

Mike was alone in his grandmother's house and was about to do the unthinkable. He broke into her safe and held his grandpa's Rolex watch in his hand. He stared at it as if he were in a third dimension. Mike could see what he was doing but couldn't believe that he was capable of it.

His 80-year-old grandmother's safe held other family heirlooms, vintage gold jewelry, and the like. The shame Mike felt left its mark on his heart, but it didn't stop him. He loaded up his pockets with the loot and went to a pawn shop. Mike's heroin addiction had taken over his life. This is what he had become: a junkie stealing from his grandma. Who would have believed that this good kid with so much potential had come to this?

All through high school, Mike was a good athlete and bodybuilder. His senior year, he broke his nose and was given a prescription for Vicodin. Although he had drunk a little during his high school days, Mike wasn't much of a partier. This was different; he fell in love with prescription pain pills with a passion.

Mike felt justified taking pills that a doctor had prescribed. He remembers thinking, "This is great. The pills make me feel euphoric and I can party all night without any worry of a hangover. My parents knew I was taking them, so what was the big deal? These things made me feel invincible." Mike didn't realize that when his prescription ran out, he would have to find another way to feel invincible and that other way would eventually lead to a needle in his arm.

Mike and his friends were all using prescription pain pills. One afternoon, Mike was with a buddy who crushed up and snorted Oxycontin. Mike's buddy told him, "They call it hillbilly heroin and it's awesome!" Mike was terrified at first but with some coaxing from his friend, he went for it and snorted one as well. Mike was overwhelmed by how good this made him feel. "I had never been in such a good mood. I started using Oxycontin every chance I got. I didn't let anything upset me; I was high all the time."

One Sunday, Mike and his same buddy went to his grandma's house. His grandma had had both knees and her hip replaced and they knew she had been prescribed pain pills. She was at church and her house was empty. Mike found her purse and inside was a bottle of Oxycontin. He stole a handful and they left. Something about it didn't feel right to Mike but that was quickly forgotten when he snorted the first pill. His grandma's multiple prescriptions would be a steady source of Oxycontin for Mike.

Mike started going to his grandma's house every few days. Soon it turned into every day. His grandmother eventually caught on and confronted him. Mike broke down into tears and confessed that he had an addiction. Neither Mike nor his grandmother knew that this would lead to a lifestyle of manipulation and to an addiction that wouldn't take no for an answer.

The secret was out, and Mike's family sent him to a drug rehabilitation facility. He was sent home after 13 days and he announced the lie that he was cured. He failed to say that his doctors had sent him home with three prescriptions of various narcotics to keep him stable. In no time, Mike was snorting these and manipulating his grandmother into giving him more Oxycontin.

A violent snowstorm was building in Mike's life but he wouldn't notice it immediately. It started with flurries one night when Mike shot up heroin for the first time. Then it blew icy cold as he learned to shoot up painkillers. There was no turning back when the brunt of the storm released its full fury, turning Mike's life sideways like a tattered flag clinging to a frosted flagpole.

Mike could no longer get high from swallowing or snorting pain pills. His high would have to be shot into his veins. Mike had become a junkie.

Mike would now steal anything his addiction dictated. He stole from his grandma, his brother, and his parents. Mike even manipulated his brother into taking a drug test for him. The results tested clean and Mike landed a great job that could have become a career. However, he was fired within three months due to his lack of accountability. Mike would get hired at a number of jobs, but then he would steal all he could before he was caught and fired. Mike wasn't allowed into his family's home without supervision by a family member.

Mike's life was in total chaos and he felt hopeless. He knew that he was in trouble and his life had become unmanageable. "I grew up Catholic and going to Sunday school. I didn't really understand all of it, but I did believe in God at one point in my life. However, I had dug a hole so deep I thought he couldn't see me," Mike recalls. "I was mad at God. I was enraged. How could he let this happen to me? It was too late for me and he wouldn't want a person like me anyway." Little did Mike know that God would return to his life and that he would come to understand that God had wanted him all along.

Mike met a girl and they fell deeply in love. She knew something was up with Mike but didn't understand the full extent of it until a dope-sick Mike showed up. He had to get high and his needle was empty. He went through some of his stuff and found an old dope spoon that he had used to burn down heroin. When burned down, heroin becomes liquid enough to be sucked up into a syringe and shot into a vein. The spoon had some residue from previous use, so Mike scraped it up, re-burned it, and shot up.

Mike became very ill immediately and was rushed to the hospital. Mike's body was septic, and it was feared that the infection had spread to his heart. The doctors couldn't be sure but if it had spread to his heart, it was time to notify the family and call the priest.

Part of being a drug addict is acting like one. Mike tried to leave the hospital and go to his drug dealer's house. He was caught by the staff and convinced to return to his room. In a few short hours, his dealer was at the hospital, shooting heroin into Mike's IV.

When Mike got out of the hospital, he told his girlfriend he couldn't go on without her. Despite his addiction, he was deeply in love with her.

They moved in together and she tried to make it work. Mike remembers, "One night she came downstairs in the middle of the night and I didn't hear her. She rounded the corner and walked into the room at the exact time the needle entered my body. She looked directly into my eyes and told me she thought she was looking at Satan."

The blackness of the evil that possessed Mike gleamed from his eyes. He sat and stared back. It was as if the evil of the universe was looking right through her. The stare caused a chill to course throughout her body. The cold of the chill made her think, 'Who is this monster that I have allowed into my life?'

At this point, Mike desperately wanted to stop. He didn't know how, and he didn't know how to live clean any longer. Mike was at a loss; his life was in shambles and his reputation was ruined. His parents lived in shame, and he knew that if he didn't stop, his addiction would take his life.

On a snowy afternoon, Mike was shoveling snow at his mother's house when he started to pray. He let down his ego and asked for God's help. Mike prayed out loud among the snowy background: "God, I don't know what to do. Will you please help me? Will you please show me?" A still, small voice deep within Mike's body spoke back. "The voice was so clear, I thought it was coming from outside of me, but it was not. It was God's voice talking to me," Mike says. This time, he was ready to listen. The voice inside of Mike spoke: "My son, you will be saved."

Mike ran into the house and said to his girlfriend, "You're going to think I'm nuts, but God spoke to me." In shock, she yelled, "What?" Mike sat down and wept, almost uncontrollably, the years of terror, guilt, and shame feeling lighter with every tear that fell. "It was God's way of cleansing me and telling me it was going to be ok."

Even after that glorious awakening, Mike admitted, "I still was using, I was still stealing, and I was still lying to my family." Then, out of nowhere, the voice spoke to Mike again: "You must confess everything, you must tell the truth." Mike obeyed the voice and confessed his sin of addiction. Mike told his girlfriend and everyone in his family what he had done. He even revealed the sources he had used to get drugs. They didn't know what to do next, so they decided to keep Mike on lockdown in his room.

During Mike's lockdown, he saw a commercial for an addiction treatment center. It played over and over in his mind. He couldn't keep it out of his thoughts, no matter how hard he tried.

The next evening, his parents came home from work and said, "Here, we wrote down this phone number for an addiction treatment center we saw on TV." Mike was speechless when he saw it; it was the same phone number he couldn't get out of his head. Mike now calls it a "God wink."

One call led to another call that led to another. With no rooms available anywhere close to home, Mike became discouraged. He soon came to realize that he wouldn't find a recovery facility locally. A local rehabilitation facility called and told Mike that they had found a 30-day addiction recovery center in Texas that had room for him.

Houston, Texas is a big city and an easy place to hide out if a person wanted to do so. Mike went to Houston to avoid hiding anymore. It was there that Mike turned over his life to a power greater than himself, and it was there where Mike was saved.

Mike recalls his awakening with perfect clarity. "I was ready, and I was willing to do whatever it took to get better. I had a bible and I had a God. I had a sponsor who held me accountable and showed me how to do the 12 steps of recovery. I admitted I was powerless over my addiction. I came to believe that a power greater than myself could relieve me from my addiction and return me to sanity."

Mike admitted to God, to himself, and to another human being the exact nature of his wrongs. This is step 5 of most 12 step recovery programs. However, he did not do this in a private or customary way; he revealed his sin to the world.

Mike was on the patio with about 30 other patients when he knew it was time to pray. The still, small voice in his head to which Mike had now become accustomed spoke clearly and loudly: "Humble yourself, my child, and know that I am God."

At that moment, Mike turned around his chair and got on his knees. He put his elbows on the chair and started praying. He didn't care how many people were around him. He closed his eyes and began asking out loud for forgiveness.

"I don't know where it all came from, but I know it was deep in my gut and it was part of me," Mike admits. "I sobbed and with every wrongdoing I admitted to, it shed another layer of guilt from my life. It must have been a half hour before I opened my eyes. Everyone had left except one guy who I found out later gave his life to God as well. That day was my tipping point and I knew my addiction would be healed."

Mike completed his 30-day recovery program and returned to Michigan. To the delight of all who knew him, his physical appearance was amazing. No one could believe how good he looked and that he was thinking with a clear and determined mind. Mike was very pleased with his new life and that his love, Ashley, was still there beside him. Mike continued his bible study and his step work but was haunted by thoughts of "Now what?"

The "now what" would come from a phone call. The caller on the other end stated, "Come to Texas." With Ashley by his side and in a beater car, Mike drove southwest to their destiny. The early struggles were real, but they not only survived but thrived. From Mike's beginnings selling roofing jobs, he and Ashley now own an enormously successful roofing and construction company in San Antonio.

Mike and Ashley are a living example of what is possible and their blessings still humble them. Mike survived the near-death experience that is heroin addiction. He went from the depths of an addicted hell to being a man of untethered faith.

They have turned their will and their lives over to a God of their understanding. I learned about Mike when he blessed us all with his story at a drug summit. I heard a local prosecutor mention him and his positive message on a radio station. I sought his story and he shared it with me. Mike used all of the 12 steps of Alcoholics Anonymous to get better and now is living all the promises. He is a walking, talking step 12 every time he shares his story. What an honor to share it.

Live free, find a 12-step program that fits your situation. Change the words to suit and do the work. You will be amazed before you are half-way through.

IN CLOSING

In closing I want to encourage you to find a twelve-step program that will work for you. Real change isn't a fad or a quick fix. It is a lifestyle that you will treasure as you grow. How wonderful it will be as you grow and lead others toward a better and more fulfilling life.

The simplest way to find the different twelve-step programs is to use the internet. Good luck along your journey.

To contact me regarding this book or for information on speaking at your event please;

call me:

Phone: +1-517-499-2951

You can also find me at these social media sites:

Facebook: Perry Watkins

Facebook: Perry Watkins Loveyoursource

Instagram: Perry.inspires

Email: perrywatkins23@ymail.com

45475110R00102

Made in the USA
Middletown, DE
16 May 2019